# DOUBLE PASS

## Books by David Chill

*Post Pattern*

*Fade Route*

*Bubble Screen*

*Safety Valve*

*Corner Blitz*

*Nickel Package*

*Double Pass*

*Tampa Two*

*Curse Of The Afflicted*

# DOUBLE PASS

A Novel By

# DAVID CHILL

*For Warren Bayless*

# *One*

Our past never really leaves us. Those distant memories may be tucked away in the dim recesses of our minds, but they are always there, just waiting for the chance to emerge again.

Sitting in my office, I listened to an angry old man prattle on about how Noah Greenland was wildly overrated. He did not have a high opinion regarding anything about Noah Greenland, which was fine, since I didn't have a high opinion of the angry old man.

Noah Greenland was, in fact, a marvelous high school quarterback who had a big arm and precision accuracy. The angry man seated across from me was an aging dilettante who was used to getting his way. His name was Earl Bainbridge and he owed me four thousand dollars, although I strongly suspected he had failed to remember that.

Earl Bainbridge was old-money Pasadena, and old-money folks decide how much they would pay someone, prior agreements being a minor inconvenience. Earl reminded me of a portly man who recently tried to hire me to dig up dirt on a former partner. That portly man was a real estate contractor, one who typically paid just a fraction of the agreed-upon fees to the plumbers, carpenters and electricians he hired. It was a sweet deal for him, not so much for the people who did the work. These people found out it was both expensive and frustrating to try to claim the rest of their money, with the episodes sometimes dragging out for years in court. Even if they won, their legal fees made the whole exercise fruitless. It was easier to simply resign themselves to not getting their final payment. After listening to him boast for awhile, I finally declined the portly man's assignment. I probably should have declined Earl's original request, too, but back then, a near-lifetime of eight years ago, my checking account was advising me that I needed an injection of money, spurious as it turned out to be.

"I don't like that Greenland family," he declared. "They're not my kind of people."

"What does that mean?" I asked.

"They don't belong at St. Dismas. The Greenlands are only there because the coaches wanted Noah. The parents have money but he's getting a full scholarship. Noah's sailing along on a free ride. That doesn't sit well with me. Plus, they live up in La Crescenta. They're not even from Pasadena."

"Noah's what they call a five-star quarterback," I pointed out, drawing upon a reservoir of knowledge gleaned from my recent stint as a football coach. "Next year he'll be playing college ball somewhere, probably starting. Kids like that don't come around often. So they get taken care of."

"He isn't that good," Earl sniffed. "Bunch of hype if you ask me."

Actually, Noah Greenland was indeed that good. But it was also true that he was showered with a lot of publicity. As a high school player, some of his games aired on national TV. He was the subject of intense recruiting among college coaches. Even the *Los Angeles Times* did an article on him, how Noah had led St. Dismas, a school with little history as a football power, to a state title last season. It was a rags to riches tale that was just too juicy for the paper to pass up.

"So what's your interest in him?" I asked. "And how does that bring you to my doorstep ... again?"

Earl Bainbridge licked his lips before he spoke. He was now in his mid-sixties, lean, tan, and had a strong, craggy face. He was sporting more wrinkles now, and an ugliness exuded from his eyes. But he still had a head full of reddish brown hair, unnatural for a man of his advanced years, a feature that had obviously been afforded full professional treatment. The colorful hair did not make him look young; it just made him look strange.

"There's been fundraising issues for the team. We've raised a ton of money, and most of it's gone now. No one's giving me an honest answer about where it went. But it's gone."

"You speak with the coach?" I asked.

"I think he's part of the problem."

"How about the principal?"

"Do I look like an idiot? Of course I spoke with the

principal. I got nowhere. They're all in cahoots."

"Maybe you should hire a forensic accountant," I suggested.

Earl shook his head. "No, and I have my reasons. This needs to be on the hush-hush. Plus, I don't want to draw unwanted attention to the team. First game is this Friday night. It's football season, our opener is against De La Salle, one of the top schools in the state. This is our coming-out party, it's going to be shown live on Fox Sports. Can't get the team distracted by any kind of public scrutiny."

I considered this. While college football had long maintained a national presence, I was surprised at the media focus that high school football was now getting, an attention that cascaded far beyond the student body and college scouts. My perception might change if our son Marcus started playing football a dozen years from now. But that was a big if. My wife Gail was worried about concussions, and was probably not going to be supportive. Fortunately, a dozen years would afford us a lot of time for discussion.

"And so you want to know where the money went," I said, thinking of my own unpaid bill from Earl. "Money's important to you. I remember from when I investigated your wife way back when."

A scowl crossed Earl's face. It actually made him look even more curmudgeonly. "You mean ex-wife. I divorced that snatch after you found her cheating on me. Don't worry. I made sure she didn't get much in the settlement. Just enough to live on, which is still more than she deserves."

I wasn't worried, nor was I surprised. People like Earl, aging layabouts, who had never done hard work in their lives, had simply inherited their oversized nest eggs and spent a portion on attorneys who would protect it. Earl had enormous wealth, but was an enormous tightwad, too. It was surprising how often the two intertwined.

"You ever remarry?" I asked.

"Of course I did. I'm on my third trip to the plate," he replied.

"So you're in-between divorces."

Earl gave me an annoyed look. "You don't need to put it that way."

"All right," I said, and tried to temper my annoyance with him. I looked out the window. It was a hot, sunny morning, the type of morning that often foretells the end of summer in Los Angeles. It was a day that came complete with a bright blue sky, but there were also some streaky clouds off in the distance.

"So your interest here is because some of the funds in the fundraising were yours," I continued.

"More than some. A lot more than some, in fact."

"Sounds like you've acquired a generous streak," I said.

"I'll take that as a compliment."

"Well, it's possible that I said it wrong."

"Look," he said. "I donate to causes that are worthwhile."

"And this one is worthwhile because ... "

"Because my son plays on the team. Austin's a senior. You mean you haven't heard of Austin Bainbridge? I thought you were a college football coach once."

"Once," I confirmed, although it was really not that long ago. My tenure coaching defensive backs at USC had ended this past New Year's Day, fittingly in the Rose Bowl Game in Pasadena. Ironically, the Rose Bowl itself was only a short walk from the Bainbridge Estate, located in what amounted to a dry creek called the Arroyo Seco. That neighborhood was also close to where Jackie Robinson had grown up. Pasadena was, and in many ways continues to be, a very eclectic community. It was a bit like Santa Monica in that regard; the city was home to the very rich and the very poor, as well as a few who were in-between.

It was highly unlikely Austin Bainbridge would ever get to play in the Rose Bowl, but stranger things have happened. I knew a little about Austin Bainbridge because I knew about Noah Greenland. At USC, we recruited Noah hard, the same way we recruited all top prep football players in the Southland. But Austin was just another kid, good but not great. And in the world of big-time college football, just being good wouldn't cut it. Not anymore.

When Johnny Cleary was head coach at USC, he wanted to erect an invisible fence around the Southern California region, corralling the top football players and keeping them from committing to far-flung schools like Alabama, Michigan or Notre Dame. So we did a full-court press on every five-star recruit, pursuing them the way the hottest girl in a school might be pursued. By the time we were done, most of these players had seen every one of our coaches at their doorstep; by National Signing Day, a lot of them had come onboard. Noah committed to the

Trojans over a year ago, right after the Nike Combine, where high school players get their athletic skills assessed. But when Johnny left USC this past January for a job in the NFL, Noah Greenland decommitted. He said he wanted to explore other offers, of which he had many. A player like Austin Bainbridge had fewer scholarship options to fall back on.

"I'm supporting my son," Earl told me. "By donating to his team. But I don't like what's happening there. Never liked that school, really."

"So why did you send Austin to St. Dismas?" I asked.

"Oh, heck, I wanted him to go to Eastridge, where my other kids went. But Austin said he wanted a crack at playing big-time football. Okay, sure, he's got that right. It's just that the more I look at this football program, the more problems I see. And I want the people in charge held accountable."

Any situation having to do with money going from Earl's wallet to someone else's would certainly not sit well with him. And he was going to do something about it. But apparently he didn't recall our last encounter.

"So how do you know there's money missing?"

"Because I asked," he snarled. "And I have a contact at Crown Bank, where the school has a number of accounts. My friend down at the club, his nephew works there. Told me that a boatload of money came in and went out very quickly. Wouldn't give any more details, said he could lose his job. Little turd. Coach Savich said they were going to buy all new equipment. New tackle sleds, punting machines, flex chutes, that sort of thing. Put in field turf.

Get new uniforms for the kids. Helmets, too, the kind with real gold in the paint."

"Oh, yeah, the real gold kind," I repeated. USC's long-time rival, the University of Notre Dame, started this trend. It wasn't enough that their team managers spray-painted the Fighting Irish helmets the night before each game. They needed to keep pushing the envelope, so they introduced gold helmets that contained real gold flakes. The result was they more resembled Christmas ornaments than anything a tough football player from years past might want to wear. But the style caught on, and soon, many programs wanted something similar. Even high school teams.

"And now they can't buy the kind with real gold, because the money's all gone," I said.

"You catch on quick," he responded dryly.

"And what do you want me to do about it?"

"Whaaa...? I want you to find out who did it, find the people responsible, for crissakes!" Earl sputtered, reminding me once again I was weary of being hired by people who come equipped with an inch-long fuse coupled with a bloated sense of entitlement. "I want justice! That's why I'm here!"

"Oh, right, justice" I said, sighing to myself. "So if you suspect theft, why don't you go to the police?"

"My goodness, man! Haven't you been listening to me?!" he practically shouted. His agitated tone had become more akin to what one reserves for shouting a drunken, late-night burger order into a scratchy drive-thru speaker.

"Sadly, yes."

Earl continued to seem flustered, but pressed on. "Then you know St. Dismas is a religious school. A private school. And this is a private matter. Filing a police report makes it a public matter. And we can't air our dirty laundry in public. Certainly not now."

No, of course he couldn't. Or wouldn't. Earl Bainbridge wanted me to comb through the dirty laundry quietly. Discreetly. "And if I find out what happened," I asked, "just what do you plan to do about it?"

"What do you think I'll do?!" he demanded.

"I can imagine a few things," I responded sharply. "And none of them sound good. Or legal."

"Look," he said with his own sigh of exasperation. "No one's going to get hurt. We only want to find out what happened."

"We?" I asked, raising my eyebrows for emphasis. Maybe I was making a little progress. Let someone talk long enough and they'll start to reveal things.

"Yeah, we. The directors. I sit on the board of that school. They invited me, they like having big donors on the board. If we find out a school employee was siphoning funds, they'll be fired. And arrested."

It would have helped if Earl had passed on that little tidbit earlier. Having a board of directors presented some legitimacy. If it were merely Earl on a lone wolf mission, I might have turned him down. Might have. There was still the matter of his age-old debt.

"I can look into it," I said, leaning back in my chair and glancing up at the tiled ceiling in my office. Time to play some poker with Earl.

"Fine."

"But I won't."

"Won't?" he said incredulously. "And just why not?"

"Because the last time you hired me to do something, you didn't pay me what you owed me."

"Of course I did," he declared. "I remember writing you a check in this very office."

"I just moved into this office in March," I pointed out.

"Well, wherever you were. I know I did."

I reached into my desk and pulled out a manila folder. Opening it up slowly, I pretended to peruse the paperwork. I had already gone through it yesterday, when Earl had called to set up the appointment. Earl had initially been referred through an old colleague at the LAPD. My tenure as a police officer had just ended in spectacular fashion, and my struggling private investigation business needed some clients. At the time I was charging five hundred a day, and Earl had paid me for two days up front, although even getting that took some haggling. But the investigation of his young wife required a lot longer than two days.

"You had me look into your ex's infidelity. I followed her around for two weeks before I caught her with another man. They were having quite a good time, if I recall."

"You don't need to remind me of the details. That's uncalled for."

"I do need to remind you that you only paid me a two-day retainer. I was never compensated for the other eight days. Or did you change your address and not get the six invoices I sent you?"

Earl took a deep breath. "You never finished the job."

"I finished the job I was hired to do. I found out your wife was cheating, who she was cheating with, along with where and when. I just wasn't going to be a full-fledged peeping Tom."

"I wanted video evidence. You refused."

"That wasn't part of the deal," I said. "You hired me to find out if she was having an affair. I did and I gave you the details. I don't do that other stuff. Directing porno films is not the way I earn a living."

"I wanted a snoop. I only got part of the job, so you only got part of the fee."

I took a good look at Earl. He represented everything I disliked about my line of work. He was a client who was arrogant, demanding and unappreciative. The Bainbridge family was part of what amounted to landed gentry in these parts. Earl's great-grandfather was one of the pioneers who helped move the West into the modern world. He was from Oklahoma, departed during the drought, and brought the family out here with nothing more than a background in farming wheat. As Los Angeles grew, he saw an opportunity and opened a bakery. It did well, so he opened another and then another. Pretty soon, Bainbridge was churning out the brand of white bread that generations of Angelenos grew up eating.

The Bainbridge Bakeries had been a family business, handed down through the generations. But by the time the mantle should have been passed to Earl, his family had turned it into the Bainbridge Corporation, a publicly traded entity, and Earl was simply a very large shareholder. Earl didn't need to run the business, all he needed to do was oversee the massive wealth that had fallen into his lap. And protecting assets was one thing Earl did remarkably well. Especially from people like me.

"And that's why I'm not doing business with you," I countered, pointing to the door. "I work for a living. I need to get paid for what I do."

Earl took a deep breath. Instead of getting up and leaving, he slumped deeper in the chair. His defiance was humbled and he suddenly looked frustrated. He thought for a moment and then spoke.

"Look," he said, "I need someone like you."

"That's funny. I don't need someone like you."

"I ... I need someone with a background in football. Someone who can do an investigation properly. There aren't a lot of snoops out there for this kind of job."

"And you can stop calling me a snoop. I'm a private investigator. And I charge fifteen hundred a day now."

Earl's eyes widened when he heard the figure. My normal fee was now a thousand a day, but I sometimes lowered it if the client was not financially secure. For people like Earl, the fee was jacked up accordingly.

"All right," he said finally, his mouth tightened, as he drew a checkbook out of his pocket. "But I want you to turn that football program at St. Dismas upside down. I want to know everything about everything."

"Sure," I said. If there was one thing I was good at, it was poking at an issue until I learned more than I anticipated. Or sometimes more than I wanted to. I wondered if Earl was prepared for that.

"You'll probably want a two-day retainer," he said. "Like last time."

"No," I said.

"No?"

"What I want is a four-day retainer, because I think I'll need at least four days to do a thorough investigation. If it's less, I'll give you a refund."

"That's six thousand dollars you want me to fork over," he said, lowering his eyes. "And I'm supposed to trust you to keep your own hours?"

"Yes. That's exactly what you're supposed to do. Don't worry. Unlike you, I'm honest when it comes to money."

Earl scowled. "You have a nasty way about you."

"Sure," I said. "And it's not six thousand dollars you'll be paying me. It's ten thousand."

"Huh?" he glowered. "Just how did you get to that? You have some awfully funny math."

"It's simple," I said. Part of me was hoping Earl Bainbridge would get up and leave. The other part wanted to get paid. "You'll also need to pay me the four thousand you owed me from before. Eight days at five hundred a day. That debt gets settled before I do any more work for you. And you should feel lucky I'm not charging you interest on the debt."

Earl's anger began to turn into bewilderment. I suppose he began to conclude this was the only way he would get to hire me, and perhaps the only way he would have a uniquely talented investigator take on the case. Resigned to this, he finally acquiesced and raised his pen.

"All right. Do I make it out to Burnside Investigations?"

"Your bank should. I'll need a cashier's check."

"Oh, come on!" he yelled, his irritation rising to a fevered pitch. "I mean, is this really necessary?"

"In your case, yes," I said. When someone cheats you out of money, their credibility is shot. I allow people to take advantage of me once. Give a cheater a second chance, and they'll have a second opportunity to cheat you.

Earl stood up, looked as if he were about to storm out, and then stopped. Resignation crept across his wrinkled face. "I imagine there's a Wells Fargo in West L.A.? I don't normally leave Pasadena. No reason to, you know."

"There's one over on Pico. Past Westwood. You can be there and back in fifteen minutes. It's mid-morning. Traffic's light."

He turned to leave, but I had one more question.

"Say, Earl."

He turned back to look at me. "Don't tell me you have one *more* requirement."

"Nope. Just a question."

"What's that?"

"How much money did you personally donate to St. Dismas for this fundraising venture?"

Earl's expression turned sheepish and he looked at me for a good five seconds. I wasn't sure if he was trying to make me sorry I had asked, or simply trying to remember the amount. "A hundred thousand," he finally said. "That impress you?"

I let out a low whistle. And I started to think my fifteen

hundred-a-day fee might have actually been too low.

"That's quite a lot."

"Yeah," he said sourly. "I wish I had never sent Austin to that school. But he's a senior now, so it's done. I should have listened to a friend of mine at the club. He told me who this St. Dismas character really was, but I just laughed it off."

"All right. So who was St. Dismas?"

"He was referred to," Earl said, a nasty sneer crossing his face, "as the patron saint of thieves."

# *Two*

Only a few minutes after Earl left, my past continued to resurrect itself, this time in the form of a willowy woman, fortyish, and mildly pretty. Her name was Rebecca Linzemeier, and for many years she had lived in the apartment below mine in Santa Monica. Ms. Linzmeier was a woman I would have rather forgotten, the unpleasant memories flooding back to me like the stench of a nasty meal that made your stomach do cartwheels. Coming on the heels of Earl Bainbridge, I decided this was not my day. I shuddered to think who else would be passing through my office door.

I was never really attracted to Rebecca, although she had made it quite plain she would welcome such an overture. And I suppose if I had not lived above her apartment for twelve years, I might have been tempted at one point. But the building we lived in had no insulation, and I think I heard every shrill conversation she ever had, and every sniveling comment she ever uttered. Rebecca Linzmeier was the neighbor from hell, the one who got up at 5:00 a.m. and felt she had the right to make a ridiculous amount of noise. The only times she slept in were when the occasional boyfriend spent the night, and her nocturnal screams were the stuff of legend. She certainly had no qualms about letting the world know just how much she was enjoying yourself. Her neighbors, myself included, suffered through it.

"Mr. Burnside," she said formally.

"Ms. Linzmeier."

"You remember me."

"I have a good memory for certain things," I said, not telling her those things were mostly ones which had ruined many a good night's sleep.

"May I sit down?" she asked.

"You may."

Ms. Linzmeier sat down, looked around the room, took a deep breath, and then burst into tears. She closed her eyes tightly, her mouth wincing and her chest heaving slightly. She tried to stop crying, but as is often the case, the harder one tries to stop doing something, the more difficult it becomes. She composed herself for a moment, apologized, and then began whimpering again. I reached into my desk and handed her a box of tissues. She took it without a word, pulled two out, dabbed her eyes and blew her nose. After another minute or so, she took a deep breath and let it out in a very pronounced sigh.

"I didn't mean to do that," she said.

"It's all right," I said. "No one ever does."

"You're probably wondering why I'm here."

"Well, yes," I said.

"It's got nothing to do with the apartment building."

"All right."

"I know you moved out a while ago," she said.

"Yes, we bought a house," I pointed out. "We're in Mar Vista now."

"I remember your wife. She was nice. So beautiful. And you had a baby."

"We did," I said, repressing a need to start tapping my fingers on the desk. "Tell me. What brings you here."

"I ... I have a problem."

"I assumed you did. What's going on?"

She took another deep breath, flinched for a moment, and successfully held off another wall of tears. "It's my boyfriend."

"What did he do?"

"I'm not sure. Not entirely sure, mind you. But I think. Well, I'm pretty sure Doug's cheating on me."

It was my turn to take a deep breath. I hated these types of cases. A partner's infidelity, like the previous occupants of your hotel room, was a subject you simply didn't want to think about. This reminded me yet again of why Earl Bainbridge had hired me back in the day. My initial thought was to advise Ms. Linzmeier that no relationship grows if it's built on a lie. But of course my potential client didn't know this for certain, and even if she did, she might not want to end things. When it comes to matters of the heart, things often get messy.

"Why do you suspect this?"

"I've found credit card receipts. From a hotel restaurant. A really nice one. Shutters. Over on Pico."

"Have you confronted him?"

She shook her head no. "I can't do that. Not without

proof. I would just feel too foolish. And what if he went and denied the whole thing? How could I possibly know for sure?"

"Are you living together?" I asked.

"Not exactly. Doug still has his own apartment. But he stays at my place three or four times a week."

"And you think he's been seeing someone at this hotel."

"I can't be sure. But it's strange. I do remember one night he came home and I smelled perfume on him. And he was drunk. And it was a night where I found a credit card receipt."

"That does sound strange," I pondered. "Can I ask what his financial situation is like?"

She blinked a few times. "I suppose it's good. He's a mortgage broker. Gets home loans for people. He's not exactly rich, but he makes a nice living. Why is that important?"

I shrugged. People who are having affairs will sometimes get a room, but Shutters was an exclusive hotel, and those who stayed there were typically doing extremely well financially. Or the people they were seeing were here on business trips and mixed in some pleasure. But if this Doug still maintained his own place, it was interesting that he chose not to use it. Maybe he just didn't want to take the chance of getting caught.

"I'm not sure if his finances are important," I finally said. "So you want me to do what here? Find out if he's actually having an affair? Are you sure you want the answer to that question?"

She agreed vigorously. "I have to know."

"What will you do if I find out he's been cheating?" I asked. Before I take on a case with emotional entanglements, I wanted to at least get a sense of what I was in for.

Rebecca Linzmeier opened her mouth for a moment but no words came out right away. As she considered my question, a confused look crossed her face.

"I suppose ... I'd have to confront him," she finally said.

"And if he admits it?"

"Well, I ... I guess I'd have to ... ask him to end it. To stop the affair."

"Is there going to be an 'or else' at the end of that demand?"

"I ... I don't know. Oh, why are you asking me this? Can't you just find out for me? And we'll deal with all that other stuff then?"

I took a breath. Therein was the problem. Clients often say they have to know the truth, but in reality they don't always want it. The answer gives them closure, but it often gives them pain. I didn't have a good response for Rebecca Linzmeier, other than it's better to know than to not know. But when someone has been unfaithful to you, a part of you will never fully trust that person again. Many people claim they can forgive and forget, but the forgiving is far easier than the forgetting. The mind doesn't always operate the way we want it to.

"Yes," I said. "I can find out for you. I'll need his name and a recent photo. And if you suspect he's going there again one night, let me know. The best course of action is to be around when it happens."

"Okay. I can get all that to you. And I generally can get a good sense for when that woman might come back. Doug usually comes up with a really lame excuse of having to meet these new clients for dinner or something like that."

"All right."

"What do you charge for your services?" she asked.

This is where I wind up losing half my potential clientele. "My normal fee is a thousand dollars a day," I said, watching her carefully and seeing her grow a little paler.

"That's ... a lot."

"I do have a sliding scale," I added. "I can lower it if you're budget is constrained."

She managed a half-smile. "That sounds like something psychologists offer."

It was not the first time I had heard that particular reference, and it usually came from people quite familiar with the process of lying on a couch, staring at the ceiling and discussing their most intimate problems with a complete stranger. I thought back to my days as a bachelor and it also reminded me of a few one-night stands.

"I have an idea," I said. "It probably wouldn't be productive for me to follow your boyfriend around all day. And I do have another client. Here's what we can do. When you sense your boyfriend is planning to go back to that hotel, let me know and I'll conduct surveillance that night. I'll charge you one hundred an hour, plus expenses. And I may only need a few hours."

She processed this for a long moment. "You're being very kind to me. I guess being a good neighbor has some value."

I processed this, too, and chose not to respond.

*

Rebecca Linzmeier departed, and I spent a little time combing through the Internet, ostensibly looking into St. Dismas, but mostly surfing aimlessly. I waited to see if Earl Bainbridge would indeed come back with my payment, or if he would hightail it back to Pasadena for another eight years. If he did choose to make good on his debt, it would take Earl less than an hour to go to the bank, make the transaction, and return with the check.

As it turned out, Earl was indeed true to his word about paying me, although it wasn't Earl who showed up with my compensation. Rather, it was a courier, who presented me with an oversized yellowish envelope that contained the cashier's check. I admired the check for a brief moment, thought wistfully about my inflated salary as a college football coach the past three years, then returned to the present and counted my blessings for the things I still had.

After depositing the money into my own Wells Fargo account, I drove my Pathfinder to The Apple Pan for a hickory burger to celebrate my two new clients. But it was now past noon, and judging by the line out the door, it appeared others were celebrating something, also. It was not only hot out today, it was very dry as well, as

September often is in L.A. Waiting outside in a long queue would quickly remove any joy I was feeling. One of our local secrets is that September is often the hottest month of the year. The month when fires were most likely to rage. And the month of September was only beginning.

The trek to Pasadena wasn't bad, thirty-five minutes of steering carefully along that serpentine road we called the 110 Freeway, before it ended and spilled traffic onto Arroyo Parkway. Pasadena was once a very beautiful little community. It had evolved into a somewhat beautiful large community. The street names were often a misnomer, as there were no lakes near Lake Avenue, and orange groves were nowhere to be found on Orange Grove Boulevard. At least when I turned onto California Avenue, I knew I was still in the right state.

Pie 'n Burger was located a few blocks off the main drag. Like the Apple Pan, it specialized in just a few dishes and had thrived for many decades. But unlike the Apple Pan, it had air conditioning and the wait was a little shorter. And when I told the hostess I was by myself, she led me directly toward a single open chair at the counter. I apologized as I slid past a few patrons, who gave me the evil eye for getting seated out of turn. I sat down, flagged a waitress, and quickly ordered. My lunch arrived a few minutes later. Everything was starting to go so swimmingly today. I began to wonder if I should buy some Powerball tickets.

I dug in. My cheeseburger was good, the slice of Dutch apple pie was good, the service was good. It wasn't quite like the Apple Pan, and I guess when you've grown up with something and eaten it for four decades, nothing else tastes quite the same. Not better, not worse, just different. As I finished, I took note of the people sitting next to me at the counter. On one side of me sat a couple discussing the float they were planning for the Rose Parade, and whether it was more practical to use blue azaleas or real blueberries in their American flag. Apparently everything on the floats had to be natural. On the other side of me sat a pair of Cal Tech students arguing whether it was more advisable to go forward into the future or go backward into history, an argument that would only become an issue if the time machine they were envisioning actually became fully functional. As I waited for the check, I felt my mind start to shut down and considered the more pedestrian problem of who would be starting at tailback when USC opened its football season on Saturday.

Walking to the cash register, I noticed a row of pies in the back and decided if I was going to announce two paying clients to Gail and Marcus, I should probably come home with some spoils. As today marked my son's first day in preschool as well, it struck me that a celebration was in order. I knew Marcus liked the new and the different, so I ordered a whole strawberry pie to go. People commented how unusual it was for a three year old to be so open to trying new things, but I think Marcus liked the shock value. We took him to his first sushi bar recently, figuring he might like *tamago*, the sweetened slice of omelet placed atop a bed of rice. What we didn't anticipate was that when Marcus discovered they had eel and octopus on the menu, he wanted -- no, demanded -- to be able to try these. I'm not fully convinced he liked them, but I knew for a fact he took delight in watching others at the sushi bar point and stare at him. He clearly enjoyed the limelight.

Class was still in session when I arrived on the St. Dismas campus a few minutes later. I walked down a tree-lined path toward the school and noticed a number of beautiful green and red parrots sitting in the trees. Many years ago, a local pet store caught fire and burned to the ground. The animals were fortunately rescued, but not some of the exotic birds, which normally sat around the store uncaged. When the flames tore through the walls, the birds narrowly escaped, and re-settled in various parts of Pasadena. Their flocks grew, and they were now part of the urban ecosphere, as well as a part of urban lore. Wild parrots are simply not something you expect to come across in Pasadena, or anywhere near L.A. for that matter.

The main building on the campus had a stone exterior and resembled a medieval castle more than a high school. A bronze statue of a biblical figure, possibly St. Dismas himself, was positioned in a grassy area near the entrance. I pushed open the front door and a sleepy-looking security guard smiled and waved me through. Maybe he remembered me as a college football recruiter, maybe he thought I was a parent, but all in all, the guard seemed unconcerned about my presence which suddenly made *me* concerned. Lax security is rarely a good thing. I gave him the benefit of the doubt and assumed he recalled me as a college football coach looking to offer scholarships to certain students. He certainly wouldn't have been expecting a shady private investigator who wanted to poke his nose into the financial irregularities of a private school's questionable fundraising arm. Unaware of exactly where to start, I walked through the building and over to the football field. At the very least, I knew where that was.

Classes were now ending, and a few players, already in their practice uniforms, had begun moving out of the locker room and onto the field. A couple of men wearing blue Department of Water and Power uniforms were inspecting the grass. Climbing up the bleachers, I recognized a number of other assistant coaches from various top-tier college programs. I sat down beside Chuck Mantle, a chatty offensive coordinator from some college in the middle of the country. It might have been Nebraska or Oklahoma or Texas; I vaguely recalled he had switched schools in the past couple of years. College assistants tend to move around a lot. I knew from personal experience that their job security was tenuous at best. Sometimes coaches got fired when their school failed to win enough games. In my case, I was let go because we were too successful. Our head coach, Johnny Cleary, took a step up and accepted a head coaching spot with the Chicago Bears. USC's new coach wanted to bring in his own staff. It is indeed possible to do your job too well.

"Hi there, Chuck," I said.

"Well, Burnside," he said with a wry smile and ran a hand through his thinning gray hair. "You come for another glimpse of Noah the Great before we steal him away from Southern California?"

"Maybe I'm here looking at Austin Bainbridge."

"Who's that?"

"Wide receiver. Wears number 19."

Mantle looked down at his notes. "Oh, right, uh-huh. I remember him now. We had been looking at another receiver here, DeMetrius Hansen, but he went down with a knee injury last week in practice. I guess he slipped on a patch of wet grass. Bainbridge, yeah. Used to play quarterback before Noah got here."

"Not as good," I said.

"No one's as good as Noah. Yeah, Austin moved to wide receiver. Decent player, but I don't know that he has the athleticism to play at our school. Might fit in with a mid-major, Fresno State, Nevada, maybe Boise. Kid's speed is questionable, he ran a 4.7 in the 40, heck, we've got linemen who run faster than that. Doesn't have a great vertical leap. We might take him as a walk-on, you always need tackling dummies. But it sounds like he wants a real shot at starting. Can't blame him. I'd rather get on the field, even if it's at Eastern Washington. Better than sitting on the bench every Saturday."

"Uh-huh," I said, taking this on and then feigning innocence. "And Noah? You think he's that good?"

Mantle snorted. "Oh, yeah. Cannon for an arm. Can throw the ball seventy-five yards. Don't need to have anything more than that to pique our interest."

"There's more to playing quarterback than just the physical aspects," I mused. "The intangibles. Quick feet, quick thinking, quick release. They're a lot harder to gauge. And if a coach misjudges a quarterback, he may be out of a job."

"Yeah, yeah, I know all that. It's a concern with Noah. But when a kid can throw a ball that far, you can deal with the baggage."

"What baggage?"

"Ah, you don't want to know. But I don't think you'd want him at SC," he winked.

"You haven't heard. I left SC when Johnny moved on."

"No," he said, the jovial tone gone. "Didn't know that. Sorry to hear. Where'd you wind up?"

"Nowhere."

Mantle turned to face me. He was a guy who would never be without a job for long. He was an expert at helping kids develop the proper mechanics for throwing a football, and more importantly, on breaking them of their bad habits. From well-meaning dads to ignorant coaches in Pop Warner, and all the way through high school, players often get bad advice on how to play their position.

"Nowhere is not a great place to be, my friend. If you're interested in moving to the best place on earth, we might be able to find a slot for you in the state of Texas. I recall you knew a thing or two about coaching defensive backs."

I smiled. I had had that opportunity to follow Johnny to Chicago and declined. "Appreciate the thought," I told him, "but I believe I'm already living in the best place on earth."

Mantle snorted. "Sure. Earthquakes, smog, horrendous traffic. I don't know why anyone would want to live in L.A."

"We manage to steal a few Texas kids away from you every year. It's not just the weather."

"Yeah, I know. And I almost socked Johnny Cleary in the nose after one of those steals. Renaldo Smith. That one still sticks in my craw."

I kept the smile on my face, maybe it got bigger. The Renaldo Smith story was legendary. He was considered the best high school running back in the nation a while ago, and every coach in America salivated over him. Colleges are only allowed to visit recruits in their home during certain times of the year, and on the first night, there were coaches from six different schools who showed up at the same time. They all managed to find their way to the front door of Renaldo's house on the outskirts of Midland, Texas. Each one wanted to be the last coach in that night, because it's a generally accepted truism that the last coach to speak with a recruit usually has the best opportunity to close the deal with him.

When the coaches began arguing about who would enter and in what order, Johnny told the group, look, he didn't care about all that. In fact, if it was all right with the others, he'd go in first, spend a few minutes with the kid and then leave. The other coaches happily agreed and continued arguing for another twenty minutes until someone noticed Johnny hadn't come out. They knocked on the door, but there was no response. Apparently Johnny had led Renaldo out the back door and they went for a long walk. They talked about the hopes and dreams a teenager has, and wound up at Renaldo's favorite burger stand. Johnny quickly tweeted it as having the best burgers in the world. By the time they got back four hours later, the other coaches had angrily departed, and Johnny was suddenly becoming the father-figure Renaldo never had. Renaldo told Johnny there was no school he'd rather play for than USC, and he committed that night. He wound up as a three-year starter for the Trojans before leaving for the NFL, as a first-round draft pick. And Johnny Cleary became a deeply hated figure in the state of Texas.

"A lot of coaches were unhappy with Johnny about that one," I said.

"I'll tell you, after that incident, we kept a lookout in every recruit's backyard."

"Once burned, twice learned. Isn't that always the way?"

"Uh-huh."

"Anyone else you're looking at here?"

"Couple of guys. That center, Blaine Schechter. They have a linebacker, Kingston. And maybe the left tackle. Dash Farsakian."

I laughed. "Dash? That's some name for a guy that probably weighs close to three hundred pounds."

"Maybe more than three hundred. Name's Dashiell. Guess his parents liked mystery novels. He's got potential. We'll need to wait and see how he performs this year."

"Good left tackles are like gold."

"Sure. Every couch potato that watched *The Blind Side* knows that now," he said and then looked carefully at me. "So what brings you here if you're not coaching anymore?"

"I'm a private investigator," I told him.

Mantle snorted again. "You mean like Rockford?"

"No."

He looked at me more seriously. "You're investigating St. Dismas?"

"That's right. Some funds have gone missing. One of the parents is ticked."

"Uh-huh," he said, rolling this over in his mind. "You'd be surprised how much of that stuff goes on. Misappropriation. You see it everywhere. Lot of dishonesty in the world."

"Really? Even in religious schools?"

"Yeah. There's no boundaries anymore."

"Sounds like you've seen a few things. Anything you could share here?"

Mantle shrugged. "Just in general. Everyone starts out real righteous, raising funds for the team. You see it more in public schools because of budget cuts, but like I say, it's everywhere. We're a pay-as-you-go society these days."

"Is that a bad thing?"

"I don't know. Maybe. Anyway, once the money starts coming in, the big plans get changed. The new scoreboard, well, maybe that's a little too expensive. Do they actually need new tackling sleds? Maybe the field can be grass for one more year instead of yanking it up and laying out that field turf crap."

"You're against field turf?"

"Do you know what's underneath that field turf stuff? Ground-up tires. That's why you see those black pellets shoot up every time a kid hits the ground. Imagine breathing that in every day."

"Okay," I said. "So plans change. What happens to the money? I mean, in general."

Mantle gave me a look. "Think about it. Who's in charge, once the cash rolls in? Sometimes you don't have to look any further than the head coach. Usually. If not him, he knows where it's going."

"Where might it go?"

"Depends on the school. Might be the principal. Once in a while an employee is skimming. But this stuff typically begins and ends with the coach."

The head coach at St. Dismas was Duke Savich. He had been coaching there for four years, and rumor had it he was looking to move on. Noah Greenland was a senior now, and when a coach loses a great player, the team sometimes buckles the following year, especially if there weren't other star athletes in the pipeline. High school coaching was now becoming like coaching in college and the NFL; a bad season or two, and you're out.

"What do you know about Savich?" I asked.

"He's got a history."

I gave Mantle a look. "That doesn't sound good."

"Complicated. He's a Notre Dame guy. Thought a Trojan like you would know that."

"I guess I didn't."

"He grew up in South Bend, got into Notre Dame more because they give preference to local kids. Made the team as a walk-on. His nickname was Rudy, except Savich never made it onto the field. Mostly worked with the scout team."

"So how's that complicated?"

"Got in trouble with the local cops there. Mostly stupid stuff, the types of things an overzealous fan might think of. When the opposing team was in town, he'd go into their hotel and pull the fire alarm at 3:00 a.m. Maybe let the air out of the tires on the other team's bus. Or go into their locker room before a game and turn the thermostat up to 90 degrees."

"Great training for being a coach," I said dryly.

"He's got a screw loose, but he actually knows football really well. Funny how the marginal players sometimes become good coaches. The top players don't understand why others can't do what they did. What comes naturally to the great ones is hard for everyone else."

There was something to what he said, but not in every case. The less talented players often studied what the stars did, trying to understand their ability to perform so well. They weren't able to emulate them because their talent didn't allow for it. But what these players learned could be very valuable in teaching others. Then I thought of Johnny Cleary, who was one of the best cornerbacks I ever saw. He also became a great coach, but he was a detail-oriented guy, always studying film, always looking for an edge.

More players began to drift out of the locker room and onto the field. Some lay down on the grass and did stretches, others began doing drills, a few tossed a football around. The coaches came out and blew the whistle and practice began. I kept my eye out for jersey number 4, Noah Greenland. He and three other quarterbacks began throwing passes to receivers streaking down the field. The difference between Noah and the others was astonishing. The other quarterbacks' throws were lofty, high-arcing balls that drifted maybe forty or fifty yards until a receiver ran under them. Noah's balls were tight spirals that went fifteen yards further and arrived a half-second sooner. Unlike the others, Noah's passes looked like they were shot out of a gun.

The practice lasted almost two hours. As it broke up, the dozen or so college scouts made a beeline for Noah Greenland. And to one of the St. Dismas assistant coaches. While there are supposedly measures in place to keep scouts from speaking to high school players during the season, often called the Quiet Period, these ordinances are routinely ignored, if not trampled upon.

In high school football, there is something called the "Bump" rule, which says college scouts can talk to players if they happen to bump into them. Or if one of the player's coaches introduces them. That a large contingent of scouts just happened upon Noah Greenland after a summer practice on his school campus was ridiculous, but when everyone breaks the rules, the rules don't really exist. And if no one from the NCAA is there to witness it, it becomes a violation that never happened.

I walked over to Duke Savich, who was speaking with an assistant. Duke was about my size, 6'0" and 200 pounds. His assistant looked closer to 6'9" and 280, and sported a crew cut. He actually resembled a refrigerator more than a human being. Both wore green shorts and gray t-shirts with the St. Dismas logo above a drawing of a warrior carrying a gold spear.

"Coach Savich," I said, sticking out my hand. "Name's Burnside. We met briefly last year when I was with SC. How are you?"

"Busy," he said, with the hint of a smile. "Especially for a Trojan coach."

"Former coach," I said. "I've left the business. Moved on."

"Well, that sounds like a good career move," the big man next to him commented, sticking out his hand. "Curly Underwood. I coach the defense."

I shook his hand and began to bite my tongue to try and keep from laughing. It was a futile exercise. "Your real name is Curly?" I smiled.

"What do you think?" he responded.

"Probably not. But maybe you should consider a different nickname. That one went the way of Whitey and Red. Don't hear it much anymore."

"My real name's Arnold," he said testily. "My dad was in the Marines. Even after he was discharged, all of us kids had to get crew cuts. The Curly name started out as a joke. Then it stuck."

"I guess it distinguishes you."

"Yeah. And everyone still calls me Curly. So that's what I go by."

Savich held out his hands. "You done giving my assistant a hard time?"

"I suppose," I said, keeping the smile pasted on my face, although noticing Curly Underwood maintained a stoic repose.

"So what can you do for me?" Savich asked.

"Well, I was wondering if I could get a few minutes of your time to discuss something. It relates to St. Dismas. Business."

"Oh?"

"It has to do with fundraising."

"You looking to donate to a worthy cause?"

"Not quite," I said slowly. "I'm a private investigator. Someone at the school hired me."

Savich looked carefully at me, the smile evaporating from his face. It was as if he were reclassifying my status in his mind. I was no longer a college coach he could josh with, but had suddenly morphed into a problem who might not have his best interests at heart.

"It sounds like you've been talking with Mary Swain," he finally said.

I shook my head. "No. Who's that?"

"My best friend," he said caustically. "So who hired you?"

"Can't say just yet. But I'm wondering if we could go talk."

"I'm tied up with the players right now," he said and then pointed to a few people loitering nearby. "Fundraising. That's Mrs. Farsakian's department. One of the team parents. Her first name's Skye. She's over there by the locker room. Blonde, big hair, big boobs. Can't miss 'em. I mean her."

Savich then gave a quick laugh at his own humor. I rolled my eyes and didn't bother to smile. I looked over and noticed Curly Underwood wasn't smiling either, he was shaking his head softly and looking down at the ground.

"Okay, Coach," I said. "But I'd still like to talk with you. I'd like to get your take on things."

Savich continued to peer at me carefully, seemingly trying to come up with something from the dark recesses of his memory bank. He finally succeeded. "Burnside. You're the one who used to be a cop once, right?"

"Yeah. LAPD for 13 years."

"I remember. Your story was all over the news. We should probably keep you away from kids."

I took a deep breath and restrained myself from unleashing a nasty response. The story he was referring to happened many years ago, the most painful chapter in my life. I was falsely accused of a horrendous crime, and even though charges were dropped, my name remained sullied. While many people had forgotten that episode, there were still a few pissants around who thought they had the right to goad me.

"It was nothing like what you read in the papers," I said stiffly. "And right now, I want to talk to you, not the kids."

"Uh-huh. Well, like I said, this isn't the best time. I'm usually free in the mornings. Stop by tomorrow. Show me you used to be a good cop. Bring some doughnuts."

I nodded, more to conclude the conversation amicably rather than agreeing to deliver a mid-morning snack to a snarky guy, especially one who went to my alma mater's rival, Notre Dame. As Savich and his assistant walked away, I noticed that my right hand was balled into a fist and starting to ache. I relaxed my hand, but the irritation remained.

# *Three*

Skye Farsakian was indeed very blonde and had very large breasts. Looking like she was in her early forties, she stood chatting casually with a few people, probably other parents. She had likely been beautiful as a young woman, she still was in a way, although the looks had faded as they inevitably do with many people. She wore a top that was a size too small, so her ample breasts stood out surreptitiously. As Coach Savich pointed out, they could not be missed.

"Mrs. Farsakian?" I asked.

"Why, yes," she said, smiling brightly with both sets of teeth. Her voice had a dreamy quality to it, a little too high-pitched, and having a decidedly coquettish tinge.

"My name's Burnside. May I have a word with you?"

"Of course," she said and excused herself from the group. We walked about twenty feet before I spoke.

"I understand you're in charge of fundraising for the team."

"I am indeed," she gushed. "We have all sorts of fundraising for the foundation."

"Bake sales?" I smiled.

"Oh, we tried that, but they don't bring in as much as the fireworks stand before the 4th of July."

"That's interesting," I mused. "I thought fireworks were illegal in Pasadena."

"Oh, they are," she smiled and winked. "We had to go down the road to Temple City. Don't want to break the law, you know."

I nodded. Fireworks were indeed illegal in Pasadena, as well as in much of California, but there were a few cities where they were allowed. What this did was undermine every other community's efforts to outlaw them, and rendered their laws ineffective. Personally, I never liked fireworks. When I was growing up, a ten year old in my neighborhood, Victor Figueroa, severely burned part of his hand when he lit a cherry bomb and then failed to toss it away in time. Fireworks displays were fine when they were run by people who knew what they were doing. All too often, that wasn't the case.

"Are you looking to donate?" she asked with a big smile.

"I don't know," I said as diplomatically as I could. "What other options are there?"

"Oh, we have the usual," she said, almost starting to giggle. "There's the Hoop-A-Thon on the basketball court, the Powder Puff Football Game between the cheerleaders. We started a rumor that the girls would play the game wearing bikinis this year. Not true of course, but boy did that help sell tickets!"

"I can imagine," I said, wondering how the invisible boundaries of good taste could be so easily shattered.

"And, of course, all the players are required to pay three

hundred dollars to join the team. I mean their parents of course, they pay the fee."

This time I felt my eyebrows going up. "Players need to pay money to be on the team?"

"Oh, it does help out. The scholarship players get an exception, of course. The other parents pitch in to cover those kids if the parents are in need."

"Are a lot of players on scholarship here?"

Mrs. Farsakian pursed her lips for a moment and thought. "Some. Maybe a third."

I did a quick calculation and that most likely included most of the football team's starters. "I guess you have some wealthy parents here."

"Oh, we do! In fact, we had our annual Spirit of St. Dismas Day in June, that's the big one of course. We rented out the Gamble House, that Craftsman museum near the Rose Bowl? You're not supposed to do parties or fundraisers there, but well, someone at the school had a connection. You know how that goes. We had a silent auction and raised almost two hundred thousand dollars that night. Some of the parents were extraordinarily generous. A lot of money poured into our foundation."

"I'm impressed," I said. "That's remarkable. Were there some plans for the money? Put in a new field?"

"Oh, well, I'm not really sure. There was talk of putting a Jumbotron in, but I think that might have been too expensive. The coaches were looking into it. They were talking about a lot of things, improvements to the locker room, practice field, equipment, that sort of thing. They have the latitude, you know."

"So Coach Savich directs where the money goes," I said, scratching my head and thinking that a new Jumbotron might cost hundreds of thousands of dollars. This wasn't the type of item they stocked at Best Buy.

"Yes, well, of course. Duke's the one in charge. But on the fundraising, I've mostly been working with the assistants on these events. Curly has been very involved this year."

"Curly. He's the one the size of a beer truck, right?"

Skye Farsakian giggled. "Yes. He's quite big, isn't he?"

"All right," I said, sensing the conversation going off on a path I didn't want to go down. I thought of something. "Can you tell me about a Mary Swain?"

"Ms. Swain? Oh, she teaches A-PUSH."

"A-PUSH?"

"Yes, that's right. Oh, it's A.P. U.S. History. Advanced Placement. My son Dashiell was in her class last year."

"Is she a good teacher?"

"Well, now, hmmm. How should I put this?" she frowned.

"You can be honest," I winked. "I won't tell on you."

"Oh," she laughed. "I didn't mean ... well, she's a good teacher, I guess, but maybe a tough teacher, too. She drives the kids hard. I know the coaches don't like her. And you know, she can be a real pain at times."

"How so?"

"When the team has an away game and the players need to leave early, she makes a big fuss. Says the kids need to study and that football is a waste of time. She's even tried to shut down the football team. Can you imagine? She thinks it's a distraction, not just for the players, but for all the students. She says it results in concussions, that football is a diversion, it causes more problems than it solves, That it takes too much time away from the kids' schooling, yada yada."

I could see where many coaches would not appreciate that. There is often a level of unease between academics and athletics at many schools, and it continues up through college. It also creates some tension in the student body. The football players are treated differently, they're often the big men on campus. The straight-A students feel left out. Of course, a few years later the tables often get turned, with the athlete sometimes stocking shelves at Home Depot, and the class nerd becoming a doctor or launching a startup company.

"So there's been some friction," I said.

"You might say. I'm just so glad my son has Jason Fowler this year for History. He teaches A.P. Euro. Jason is such a doll. Wonderful teacher, wonderful person. I wish Dash had Jason as his teacher last year. Instead he was stuck with that ... woman."

I had an idea. "So where might I find this woman, Mary Swain. She's probably gone home by now?"

"Oh, I doubt it. Ms. Swain stays late. She's the Chair of the Social Studies Department. She's often the last person to leave. Doesn't have much of a personal life as I hear it, they used to call women like that spinsters back in the day. But I guess not so much anymore. Mr. Mularkey, the principal, used to joke he's going to give her a key to the school. One that actually works."

I smiled and thanked Mrs. Farsakian. Walking back into the school building, I went down a long corridor connecting the athletic facilities with the main school building. That odd school smell wafted into my nostrils as I strolled through the quiet, empty hallways, passing a large banner promoting Friday night's game against De La Salle, with an encouraging *Go Warriors!* on it. After a while, I found my way to the social studies wing. Sure enough, there was a light on in the corner office, the one with *Social Studies Department* engraved on the door. But the person on the inside wasn't who I was expecting.

Instead of a bookish woman, I came upon a handsome young man in his early thirties, lean, with dark, curly brown hair. He wore a checked, short-sleeve dress shirt, and a dark, nondescript tie. He was hunched over a desk and sorting through a mess of papers spread out haphazardly around his desk.

"Hello," I said. "May I interrupt?"

He looked up from a pile of papers. "Yes?"

"The name's Burnside," I said, walking in and handing him my card.

"A detective," he mused, giving it a long look. "Well, that's certainly interesting."

"Technically, I'm a licensed private investigator. But it's easy to confuse the two."

"I suppose."

"I'm looking for Mary Swain," I said.

"Well, she's gone. And she won't be coming back for a while."

"Oh?"

"I'm Jason Fowler. Yes, Ms. Swain went out on a sabbatical. Just filed today. Odd that it happened right at the start of fall classes. I'm trying to scramble and get things together."

"May I?" I asked and pointed to one of two hard yellow wood chairs facing him. The office was bare bones, a standard gray metal desk, a file cabinet, and a few uncomfortable chairs. Some beige paint on the far wall had developed cracks. A small window overlooked a courtyard. It was September, so it wasn't close to getting dark yet, but a few soft gray shadows had begun to creep up against the stone exterior. He motioned for me to sit.

"How long have you been at St. Dismas?" I asked.

"Most of my life it seems," he smiled widely, revealing some big white teeth. "I graduated from here almost fifteen years ago. Went to college and came back. Prodigal son returns."

"Sounds like *Welcome Back Kotter*."

He laughed. "Maybe a bit. I love teaching here. But it was disturbing to see Ms. Swain leave so suddenly. She was my social studies teacher when I was a student. I decided to follow her into education. After I had a career detour that is. First, I had to spend a year in law school. Worst year of my life."

"It takes a special person to be a lawyer," I said, thinking of my wife Gail, and her job as a prosecutor with the City Attorney's office. "But great teachers are special, too."

"Yes. Mary was one of them. When I went here, the school was in transition. The don't-spare-the-rod theory wasn't working, I saw it up close. Kids who misbehaved were practically tortured."

"How so?"

"Well, there was one kid I went to school with who was disrespectful, so the teacher taped the kid's hands to his desk. Periodically the teacher would walk over and smack his knuckles with a ruler."

"I don't imagine that worked so well," I said, thinking this technique was not unlike the punishment I observed some coaches doling out to players who didn't work hard at practice. I never saw a player beaten, but coaches would sometimes require certain ones to run wind sprints until they collapsed. Or repeatedly go through the Oklahoma drill, which was a brutal one-on-one blocking exercise, forcing a player to keep doing it until they couldn't defend themselves any longer and would repeatedly get knocked to the ground.

"No, it didn't work at all," he said. "At best it created an angry kid who had to hide his emotions. Trust me, none of those kids who were disciplined in that manner turned out okay. But that was then. Tail end of an era. The old guard was shunted off and they began bringing in real teachers. Things are a lot better. It's a more nurturing environment now."

"All right."

"So how can I help you?" he asked.

"Well, I was hoping to speak with Ms. Swain. One of the parents asked me to look into some fundraising irregularities."

"Oh?"

"Apparently there are allegations that some of the money raised for the football team hasn't been dispersed properly."

"How much money?"

"I'm afraid it goes into six figures."

Fowler whistled softly and thought about this for a minute. "I'm surprised," he said. "And maybe a little shocked. What you're telling me is extremely disturbing. This is not something that looks good for a school. Especially one with a religious affiliation."

"I can imagine," I said, although my experience with religious schools was mixed. They did some wonderful things. But in high school, we played a number of football games at parochial schools. In a few instances, the clock was stopped for no reason when our opponent was trailing late in the game. Time outs were not always recorded properly. Referee calls were curiously changed by a more senior official. One of our coaches was flagged for unsportsmanlike conduct for politely questioning a referee's interpretation of the rules. Even in college, the running joke at USC was that when we visited South Bend, Indiana, to play Notre Dame, we needed to beat them by two touchdowns just to get out of there with a three-point victory.

"How well do the football coaches get on with the teachers here?" I asked.

"Oh, it's fine," he responded with a wave of the hand. "We all want what's best for the school. And the kids, of course."

"You never had any disagreements with the coaches?"

"Oh, we've butted heads a few times, sure. But the football team brings a lot of publicity to the school. Without it, most people would never have even heard of St. Dismas."

"Have you had many football players in your classes?"

"Sure."

"Mind if I ask you about them?"

"I guess not. If you think it will help."

I wasn't entirely sure it would help, but I figured the more I learned, the closer I might get inside of this fundraising issue. I didn't know a lot, so there was no great place to start.

"Noah Greenland?"

He smiled. "Ah, Noah. Everyone's hero. The captain of the ship."

"What do you think of him? I mean away from football."

Fowler stopped smiling and his face briefly revealed a grimace. "He's doing the best he can," he said slowly. "Noah's extremely bright. But he's never struck me as being very happy. Kid like that, you'd expect him to be the big man on campus. Everyone wants to be his friend. But for Noah, it always seemed like a burden."

"How about Austin Bainbridge?"

Jason Fowler sighed. "Wow. Polar opposite of Noah. Wild child, not a care in the world. He just floats through school. Austin was in my American History class last year. I don't think he handed in a single assignment he wrote on his own. Intellectually lazy. He was fine with letting girlfriends do his homework, or copying things straight from an Internet site. He didn't even bother to change a word, that's how uncreative this kid is."

"A few people might call that plagiarism. At some schools, that's justification for expulsion. Did you confront him?"

"Of course," Fowler said. "And he had the temerity to insist the Internet site copied from *him*. And when I saw one of his girlfriends hand him the homework assignment, he insisted she was only reading it out of curiosity."

"You speak to his parents?"

"Oh, boy. They're another story," he sighed. "One of the downsides to private schools is that some kids get by because of their family. Austin's father donates to the school. His parents are divorced, the mother is uninvolved. I've never seen his father come to school for anything besides football games. Can you believe that?"

Knowing Earl Bainbridge, I could believe anything. "So Austin gets away with things."

"At most, Austin gets a slap on the wrist. I know Ms. Swain was very upset about all this. She felt the whole emphasis on sports demeaned the school."

"What do *you* think?" I asked.

"Look, this was something Mary and I disagreed about. She thought football was evil. I thought it added to the high school experience. Maybe it had to do with my going here a few years back. St. Dismas wasn't always such a football powerhouse."

"What changed?"

Jason Fowler peered at me. "It was after I left. We got a new coach. Very aggressive guy, recruited some good athletes. Turned the program around. I'm surprised you didn't know this."

I frowned. I hadn't paid much attention to high school football until a little over three years ago, when all of a sudden it became my whole world. I knew St. Dismas was a big-name football factory, and I had merely assumed it always had been.

"I'll guess that's not Duke Savich you're referring to."

"No, he came in about four years ago."

"Did that other coach move on to a bigger program? Coaching in college?"

"No, in fact he's been prohibited from coaching for a number of years. That was part of the terms of the settlement with the school."

"Settlement?"

"Yes," Fowler said. "There was an altercation and a big lawsuit that followed. Some dad was angry that his kid wasn't getting enough playing time so he confronted the coach. Words were spoken, and well, the parent left the coach's office head first. The coach literally through him through the door."

"And the name of this coach...?"

"Yes, that's what's so interesting. It's Bob Greenland. Noah's dad. Sorry. I thought you knew about it."

*

The drive back to West L.A. was long, and in rush hour, there are few clear arteries. Whether crossing the valley floor through Burbank or driving into the nightmarish four-level interchange above downtown, getting home from Pasadena was a nuisance. I consoled myself by thinking of the check I had finally received this morning for an eight-year-old case, as well as the fact that I was layering an extra premium onto Earl Bainbridge. When someone makes a six-figure donation and doesn't know where the money has gone, it struck me that I could put his money to more practical use, like making some mortgage payments. It certainly wouldn't be going toward a Jumbotron.

Our house was located in Mar Vista, a few miles from the ocean, and just blocks off of Venice Boulevard. Gail and I liked that we were close to freeways, but nestled in a nice, secluded tree-lined street. The area was developed during the 1950s, so there was mature landscaping and we had a large maple tree towering over our front yard. Back East, when the cool weather set in during late September, the maple leaves would begin turning into beautiful shades of red, orange and gold. In L.A., these leaves might start to change colors around Christmas. Right now, our maple looked like any other shade tree, except this one had a gaggle of plastic balls strewn about the trunk. Few things could surpass the joy of knowing children had been playing there. I walked into my house, and it didn't take long for me to be showered with my favorite sound of the day.

"Daddy's home!"

Marcus raced over to hug my leg, and I ruffled his hair with one hand, the other hand working overtime to prevent a pie box from tipping over. This was my new life and I loved it. I had no idea I would become a father in my 40s, but my path in life had been altered by so many twists and turns, I had finally stopped planning and surrendered to the winds of fate. At USC, I had been a four-year starter at free safety on the football team, and I cultivated dreams of playing in the NFL. Those dreams came crashing down in an instant, when a freak knee injury sidelined me, and I was unable to perform for pro scouts at the Combine or at USC's Pro Day. My coach, Bulldog Martin, arranged for a tryout with the Rams, but they were already well-stocked at safety, and I was waived after the first preseason game. Little did I know I would go on to have a career as an LAPD officer, or that my subsequent departure from the force thirteen years later would be even more unexpected and painful than the knee injury.

"How was preschool today?" I asked. "Your first day at Grand View."

"Um. Okay."

"That's good."

"Well, maybe not," he managed as I peered at him. "Oh. I don't know."

"That covers most of the options," I said as Gail walked into the living room and gave me a kiss. I looked at her beautiful face and said, "I hope your day had more clarity."

"It was fine. I'm working on a new burglary case at the office," she said, smoothing her long, chestnut brown hair away from her face. "Say, what's in the box? Looks like a treat."

"A treat indeed," I said and turned to Marcus. "You think you'd like to sample some strawberry pie for dessert?"

"Oh, wow!" he exclaimed as his eyes grew wide. "I didn't know they made that!"

"Errr ... Marcus," Gail said, bending down and giving him a stern look. "Is there something you'd like to tell your dad?"

Marcus looked forlornly down at the carpet. "Do I have to?"

"Yes," she said. "We don't keep secrets from each other in this household."

"What happened?" I asked, sitting down on our couch. Marcus climbed into my lap.

"We were playing this new game I learned. Bumper tag."

"What's that?" I asked.

"It's like tag, you're it. But you have to bump them to tag them."

"Okay," I said, not sure I liked where this was going.

"So this kid named Ricky bumped me hard. And I bumped him back."

"And?"

"That's it," he said.

"Marcus ... ?" Gail said. "What else?"

"I don't remember."

I shook my head. In thirteen years on the police force, the "I don't remember" line was quite possibly the one uttered the most. Hardened criminals knew there were few benefits to cooperating with police, and they usually disseminated as little information as possible. 'I don't remember' was that type of response that would make cops furious.

"So," Gail said, picking up the story. "Ricky bumped Marcus a couple of times, and one time he fell down on the pavement."

"Uh-huh," I said, vaguely remembering a parenting advice book that said something about the blessings of a skinned knee.

"But then Marcus got up and punched Ricky in the face."

"Oh, really?" I said, becoming very sure I didn't like where this was going. "What did the school say?"

Gail frowned, and a cross look appeared on her pretty face. "The school. Yes. I spoke with the director. They warned us if it happened again, Marcus could be expelled."

I inched back on the couch and put my arms around Marcus and hugged him slightly. Part of me wanted to high-five him and tell him good job. Someone pushes you, you push them back. Someone knocks you down, you go and knock them down. I had a funny feeling though, my better half wasn't going to be pleased with that approach, and I needed to tread cautiously.

"That seems a bit harsh. Expelled from preschool?"

"It's what they told me. Some preschools have a zero tolerance policy. We're actually lucky."

I wasn't feeling lucky. I wasn't feeling very good at all. "At least we didn't spend a bundle on that Applewood Preschool. Be hard to get our tuition money back."

Gail shot me a glance. "It's not funny. I don't like this behavior in a three year-old. And I wonder where he picked it up from."

I didn't need to be a psychic to sense when an argument was coming on, and I clearly did not relish the possibilities. Gail and I had been married for over four years and I could only recall a couple of times when we even bickered. We had enjoyed quite a long honeymoon, and we both took great pains to avoid bringing the stresses of our high-pressure jobs home with us. And I had some added incentives to avoid fighting with Gail. While I could trade quips with anyone, being snide with my normally lovely wife did not hold much upside. And I also knew that arguing with a lawyer was often a futile exercise. I had motivation to settle matters maturely right now.

"Okay," I said, raising my hand in acquiescence. "You need to know, I do not encourage Marcus to fight. I have not done so. Not at all."

"But I've seen you show him how to throw a punch. And when he's mad, you'll hold up your palms and let him punch your hands. Practice."

"It's not practice," I insisted. "I want him to blow off steam when he's mad about something. And punching my hand seemed like a good alternative."

"And look where we are," she countered.

"It wasn't my intention. I can assure you."

"He has to learn to use his words when he's mad. And to blow off steam in a different way."

"Okay, we'll work on it," I said, putting Marcus down

and walking into the kitchen. I wondered how to help Marcus find another way to blow off steam. I also wondered what was for dinner. I wondered if I would be docked dessert. I also wondered if I'd be sleeping on the couch tonight.

*

I rocketed out the door the next morning, well before the clock struck 7:00 a.m., and as such, the sun was up and the traffic was fast. If I had lounged about for another 30 minutes, my commute to Pasadena would have sagged into a long, dreary slog. And if I had indeed waited that additional, prescient half-hour, Gail would be up. And I would, in no uncertain terms, have been reminded of our chilly conversation last night.

I found a Starbucks on Colorado Boulevard., not far from the Norton Simon Museum, and I settled in with a *grande* Sumatra. Around me sat a patchwork quilt of what appeared to be college students, entry-level I.T. workers, some retirees, and a few people who were likely unemployed and in dire need of getting out of the house. After waiting until 9:00 a.m., by which time classes should have started, I headed over to the high school.

St. Dismas was a short drive from Starbucks. Everything seemed like it was a short drive in Pasadena. There was traffic, but it was mild. There were a lot of stylish office buildings, but not a lot of the congestion that often comes with it. Pasadena struck me as a nice small city. Or maybe a nice big town. Almost as livable as Mar

Vista. But the temperatures were much higher here and the air was smoggier. And no amount of charm can make up for discomfort. If you're going to live in paradise, it's best to not see what you breathe.

A different security guard from the one on duty yesterday greeted me as I walked into the main building, but the reception was much the same. He offered a lazy smile and asked if I were a parent. I smiled right back and told him I was, leaving out one crucial detail. My child was not matriculating at St. Dismas High in Pasadena, but rather, was a brand-new enrollee in the Grand View preschool. At least for the time being, and pending good behavior. The guard happily waved me on in. Nodding pleasantly at each other, we both went about our jobs.

I walked over to the administrative offices of the school and asked if I could speak with the bookkeeper. I wasn't entirely sure whether I could get anything out of them, but it was worth a shot. I was told the bookkeeper's name was Ms. O'Hara, but no one knew where she was. I casually glanced at some papers on her desk, but nothing resembling fraud jumped out at me. Then a deep voice came from behind.

"May I help you, sir?"

I turned to see a tall bespectacled man with a long neck and a brilliantined comb-over looking at me suspiciously. He wore a dark suit, and he maintained an aura of authority. He did not look happy.

"Just trying to find the accountant," I smiled.

"If you're dropping off a tuition check, I can take it," he said.

"No. Actually I had a few questions for her."

"Anything I can answer?"

"To whom do I have the pleasure?" I asked, attempting to come off as easygoing, and most likely failing.

"I'm Ed Mularkey. I'm the principal here. What does this concern?"

I smiled politely. I had planned to speak with Principal Mularkey, but didn't expect much. Underlings are more likely to let things slip, and when your goal is to have subjects spill secrets, the higher up they are on the totem pole, the less prone they are to reveal much. I suggested we adjourn to the principal's office, but he demurred, at least momentarily.

"First tell me what this is about," he demanded.

"Fundraising," I said, purposely omitting words like fraud, theft, or even the decidedly squishy term, irregularities. "I'm a private investigator. One of the parents here is very concerned about what happened to their donation."

Mularkey did not hesitate, and whisked me into his office with a sweeping gesture from a very long arm. Once inside, it was quickly obvious that the principal had far more luxurious digs than the teachers or staff. His office was outfitted with an intricately designed Persian rug, the walls were freshly painted, and there was a pair of impressive teak bookcases. The smooth spines told me that many of the books had probably never been opened. A large picture window, framed with long, straight maroon drapes, looked out onto the front grounds, lush and green.

"Tell me what's going on with the fundraising," Mularkey said, getting right to the point.

My first reaction might normally have been to inform him I'd be the one asking the questions. But I sensed joviality was not one of the principal's finer traits. Mularkey had a serious air about him, one that bespoke a busy man who would appreciate neither digs nor disrespect of any kind.

"One of the donors to the football program has concerns about where his money is going."

"And who might this donor be?"

I took a breath. It wasn't wholly ethical to reveal a client, but I had the distinct feeling our conversation would cease immediately if I failed to be cooperative. And given Mularkey's omnipotent ability to limit access to anyone entering the school, my investigation might be stopped cold. But I also had an inkling that the Principal might already know who this was.

"One of the team parents," I said. "And a major donor. The type of man who writes a six-figure check without blinking. I'm sure you have some wealthy families here, but I also think you know who I'm talking about, don't you?"

Mularkey sighed. "That must be Bainbridge."

"Must be," I said, patting myself on the back for not actually confirming his name.

"Good heavens. That man is a blessing and a curse."

"How's that?" I asked.

"You know about his son."

"I know he goes to school here. And he plays football.

And rumor has it he studies once in a while."

"If that. Look, Austin came here to play quarterback. He was a good player. Not outstanding, but he'd do. Then we had a shot at Noah Greenland. That changed everything. I didn't think Noah would come at first. His family situation is, well, complicated."

"I understand his father coached here. Then he got dismissed. For cause."

Mularkey paused for a moment. "You've done your homework. Yes, he was terminated. At the time, we didn't have any idea Bob's son would become a great athlete. But he did. Noah had a brief stint in public school, but things weren't working out there. Bob asked if Noah could transfer to St. Dismas. I gather Coach Savich had cultivated a relationship with the family."

As odd as it might sound, recruiting football players often starts well before high school. Kids begin playing Pop Warner, the talented ones are recognized, and private schools will offer scholarships. The cost is often worth it; the good publicity can put some schools on the map. A few high schools have even developed national reputations because of their sports teams. But coupled with that public presence is an ongoing pressure to win. And that meant continuously recruiting new players.

"So that was the end of Austin's career as a quarterback. I'm sure Earl wasn't pleased."

"To say the least. And the fact that Noah was on scholarship unnerved him even more. You'd be surprised how wealthy people can be very petty when it comes to money."

I thought of the eight years it took Earl to pay my bill. "Maybe not."

"Anyway, Austin moved to wide receiver. He's a starter, and he's accepted his role. His father, on the other hand, is less accepting."

"I take it Earl doesn't like Savich much," I said.

"Earl doesn't like anyone much. But he detests the coaches in particular. Hates them with a passion. Any opportunity he has to snipe at them, well, he takes full advantage."

"So you're not surprised he went out and hired someone like me to look into things."

"No," he said wearily. "Earl's been making threats, but he's been doing so for two years. Looks like he's finally following through. That man needs more to do with his life."

"Perhaps," I said, not feeling any strong need to disagree. "But why not just tell him about the fundraising and how it's spent? If the guy's been writing six-figure checks, doesn't he have a right to know where his money's going?"

Mularkey sighed again and shook his head. "We can't have parents this close to school business. There has to be some separation. We appreciate parent contributions, but that doesn't give them unfettered access to how we run our school. We'd have anarchy otherwise."

"I understand," I said. This made some sense. Allowing everyone input can indeed lead to chaos, and not everyone would be happy in the end. Group decision-making can be an ugly thing. Many years ago, a minor league football team in Ohio experimented with an interactive TV technology that would allow fans to call the plays for their home team. It was interesting for a few minutes, but when the home team fell behind, the fans panicked and began voting to throw a deep pass on every play. These plays rarely worked, as the opposing team quickly caught on and installed a scheme to defend it. The game took six hours, the wide receivers were completely exhausted by halftime, and the home team got clobbered. It was an experiment no one wanted to try again.

"So what do you have so far?" he asked.

"Nothing. I don't know who to ask or what to ask them. I've spoken to a few people so far. No one knows anything. So I feel like I'm going down a blind alley wearing ear plugs."

I thought I saw a faint smile briefly cross Mularkey's lips. Then it disappeared just as quickly. "I don't think it benefits anyone for you to continue this investigation," he finally said.

"Look," I said testily, "I'm being paid to do a job. I'm going to do it. I can always contact these people outside of school. This only makes it more convenient. It sounds like someone has something to hide."

At that point, a very loud siren-like alarm started to go off. Mularkey and I looked at each other and walked quickly out into the hallway. A middle-aged woman, possibly a teacher or an administrator, raced up to us, her arms extended, and she was practically panting.

"Mr. Mularkey! The school's on lockdown!"

"What?" he exclaimed. "On whose authority?"

"The police. There's been an incident and 9-1-1 was called. The police told us to lock all the classrooms. I so can't believe this happened!"

"Can't believe what, Mrs. Cook? What happened?"

"There's been a stabbing!" she cried.

"Who?! Who was stabbed?!" exclaimed Mularkey.

"It was a faculty member. It was ... oh my God! It was Jason. I mean, Mr. Fowler. It's terrible. He's dead. He was so nice and so popular. Who on earth could have done such a thing?"

## *Four*

It took a few hours for the Pasadena police to assiduously comb through the campus and declare the grounds secure. But after listening to the murmurs of students outside of the building, it was plain that no one felt safe. The school wisely suspended classes for the remainder of the day and instructed everyone to go home. Everyone, that is, except for those special students who played on the varsity football team, who would be required to stay and attend practice. There was, after all, a big game looming on Friday night.

Many students loitered outside the campus, waiting for a parent in a foul mood to pick them up. In addition to the parade of vehicles from the medical examiner, the county coroner's office and local TV news crews, the street in front of the school was lined with black and white patrol cars from the Pasadena Police Department. Most of them were parked haphazardly, in the notorious cop style. The cruisers were angled in such a way that the rear end of the vehicles invariably protruded back onto the street. Anyone trying to navigate through the maze of black and whites needed to weave carefully around them.

I noticed a clump of muscular teenagers standing under a large oak tree. They all wore forest green t-shirts with the name *Warriors* emblazoned in gold across the center, right above the caricature of a bending goal post. Using my carefully honed detective skills, I deduced they were football players. I scanned the area to see if I could find any who weren't part of the group, and came across a familiar face. While he wasn't wearing the standard green t-shirt, I knew he was an integral part of the team. He was intently focused, looking down at his phone with a sense of urgency as I approached. Fully engrossed in what he was doing, and plainly unaware I was standing right in front of him, I needed to utter a brief clearing-of-the-throat cough to get his attention.

"How are you doing there?" I began, taking a glance around the make sure there weren't any coaches nearby.

Noah Greenland looked up quickly from whatever critical endeavor in which he had been engaged. "Oh," he said. "Hi. Okay, I guess. Do I know you?"

"You may not remember me, but I was part of Johnny Cleary's staff at SC. We met once. Briefly."

"Uh-huh," he said, appearing a little bewildered. "I sure remember Coach Cleary. You look a little familiar."

"I can imagine. Sorry to hear you decommitted from SC. Understand, new coaching staff and all."

"Right. My dad wasn't crazy about the new coaches. Said he didn't know anything about them. Wanted us to take our time."

I agreed. "It's a big decision. Don't sign your letter of intent unless you're sure it's the school for you."

"My dad is kind of handling that."

"Oh?" I said. "You're the one who's going to college, right?"

"Uh-huh. But it's kind of tough to figure out. I've had over a hundred schools offer me scholarships. They all say the same things, make the same promises, say how they're the best, tell me how they only recruit players who want to compete, whatever. My dad's taken me to visit some of them. It's hard for me to tell them apart. They all kind of look the same after a while."

"Sounds like you're not enjoying this process much," I noted. "For a lot of players, visiting different colleges is a great experience. Everything is open to you, everyone is welcoming. Trust me, when you step onto campus as a student-athlete, things change."

"What do you mean?"

"Coaches that once told you how fantastic you were, and acted as though you're the greatest thing since sliced bread, are suddenly barking orders at you like you're an army plebe, screaming when you make a mistake. Once they've got you in the fold, they go back to their normal ways. What you're seeing now is their best side. They're selling themselves to you. If you win a national championship, you might see that side again."

He managed an unhappy laugh. His expression was that of a puzzled child struggling to solve long-division problems in his head. Noah Greenland was a good-looking teenager, tall, strong, freckle-faced, with short red hair that almost resembled a lawn that had just been mowed. His features were unusual, the red hair complemented by blue eyes, the square jaw offset by a long, aquiline nose. But the one impression that kept shining through was this sadness, a sense that the weight of the world was pressing down on his shoulders, his stardom a burden rather than a blessing.

"I'm kind of used to that," he sighed. "I'm seeing it with my coach now."

"Savich?"

"Yeah. I transferred here two years ago. After freshman year. They offered me a scholarship. Coach Savich treated me like a prince during recruiting. Then I came on board. When I threw an interception in my first game, he damn near tore my head off. It's like dude, chill, these things happen."

"You finally get used to it?"

"I suppose. But I can't say as I like it."

"No one likes getting yelled at. You know, there used to be a coach in the NFL named Paul Brown. Long, long time ago. Brown had a star player who would get upset when he got yelled at. So when the coach was mad at his star, he went over and yelled at the guy sitting right next to him, usually a bench-warmer. Got the message across without hurting the star's feelings. Weird, but it worked."

Noah Greenland smiled briefly. "I'd have hated to be that bench-warmer," he said, showing a surprising amount of sensitivity. He looked up at me in a curious way. "Why'd you leave SC?"

"Not my choice. Johnny Cleary went to the NFL and the new coach wanted to start fresh with a new bunch of assistants. College sports is a business. Things change."

The smile vanished from Noah's face. "So's high school nowadays. We've got De La Salle coming in to play on Friday. Someone told me they actually have a betting line on the game. It's freaky."

"Yeah. Look, try not to let this stuff get to you. Practice hard, play hard, enjoy what you can enjoy," I advised him. "This period in your life will go by faster than you think. You've got the talent to get to the NFL. That's when things get challenging."

"I guess," he shrugged.

"Is that what you want to do?"

"I wouldn't mind being rich," he responded, with slightly more enthusiasm then he'd shown throughout the conversation. "It's tough seeing people struggle. With money, you know."

"Sure," I said, not entirely certain where this was coming from. I decided to change the subject and pointed to the school. "So tell me something. This incident that happened this morning. Did you ever have Mr. Fowler for a teacher?"

"I was in his class this semester. A.P. Euro."

"What'd you think of him?"

Noah shrugged again. "It's only been a couple of weeks. He was okay, I guess."

"Any thoughts on who might have done this?" I asked casually.

Noah looked off in the distance for a moment. "Could have been a lot of people."

"Really?" I said, resisting the temptation to ask for names. "I met Mr. Fowler. Struck me as a nice guy."

"Yeah, I think that might have been the problem. Lot of girls thought he was nice. He'd flirt with them all the time. Even in class. Tease them a little. Couple of my teammates didn't like it."

"He was flirting with their girlfriends?"

"Not so much that. They just didn't like him flirting with any girls. It was kind of like, you know, go after a woman your own age. Leave ours alone."

I frowned. "You think Mr. Fowler was actually involved with any of the girls?"

Noah looked down. "I don't know for sure. But a lot of the girls liked him. Wouldn't have surprised me. There were rumors. But hey. It's high school. You know."

"Any names?" I asked, unable to resist the temptation any longer, and also knowing I was stepping out-of-bounds here. I was no longer on any police force, but I still maintained a healthy curiosity.

"I don't know. I'd be just guessing."

I was about to tell him to go ahead and take a guess, but a middle-aged woman approached at the most inopportune moment and called Noah's name. She was slender, and had red hair that was cut short and parted to one side. She wore a teal blue pantsuit and a white top, and looked like a polished professional.

"Hi, Mom," he said, glumly, looking like he'd rather be elsewhere.

"Honey, are you all right?"

"Sure. Someone else died today. I'm fine."

The woman stopped and stared at him. "That's a terrible thing to say, Noah. Why would you even think of saying something like that?"

"I don't know."

The woman continued to stare at him for a long moment and then turned to me. "Hello," she said. "Are you with the school?"

I took a breath. "No, I'm sorry. I'm not," I said and handed her my business card. "Name's Burnside. I'm a private investigator. I'm looking into something. Unrelated to what happened today. I hope so, anyways."

"Oh," she said. "Oh, my. Why are you talking with Noah?"

"Mom. Please."

"No, no, honey, I want to find out."

"Look, Mrs. Greenland," I began.

"Dr. Greenland," she corrected me. "I'm a psychotherapist."

"Doctor, then," I continued. "I met Noah last year when I was coaching with USC. I'm not with the team anymore, I've moved on. I was just chatting with Noah. Catching up. That's all."

"And you're a private investigator now? What are you investigating?"

I looked at Noah and then back at her. She was moderately attractive and Noah resembled her quite a bit. But while her son was shy and considerate, her manner was off-putting and I didn't like it. I wasn't surprised Noah didn't like it much, either.

"I'm happy to speak with you about it," I said, my eyes surreptitiously darting to Noah. "But this isn't the best time."

She concurred. "No, I suppose it isn't," she said and turned back to her son. "Noah, come on. I'll give you a lift home."

"I can't," he said. "Coach says practice is still on."

Dr. Greenland's jaw dropped. "After what happened here today?" she asked, incredulously.

"I don't make this stuff up, Mom," he said, throwing his hands in the air and walking over to the group of football players. He didn't blend in with them, rather, he stood on the outskirts of the group and resumed looking down at his phone. His mother stared at him for a long moment before stalking off and not bothering to say goodbye to me.

I did notice, however, that Dr. Greenland stopped to talk with a few other moms, one of whom was Skye Farsakian. Quite naturally, all of them looked upset and wore worried expressions. I would have liked to speak with Mrs. Farsakian again, but decided to wait until she was alone. I began feeling a little self-conscious standing by myself, but that feeling was about to change.

A pair of rumpled detectives stood near the curb, their identities made obvious by the shiny gold shields clipped to their belts. They wore identical short-sleeved shirts and cheap, narrow ties. They were both looking straight at me, and one was pointing a finger in my direction as he spoke into a cell phone. One was short and stocky, the other was of average height, average build, and had an average face. The average detective looked like he might have a budding career as an extra in movies one day. They finally approached.

"You Burnside?" asked the short, stocky detective, who, upon closer inspection, was sporting a pencil-thin mustache.

"I am. How'd you know? My picture on the post office wall or something?"

"Wise guy, huh? No, Principal Mularkey pointed you out. Said you've been snooping around campus the past couple of days. He thought it was suspicious."

"Lots of things around this school are suspicious," I countered. "In fact, the more I look, the more suspicious it all gets. Even you two look suspicious."

They glanced incredulously at each other. The stocky detective spoke again. "You got quite an attitude for a person of interest."

I stared back at them. A person of interest was police-speak for a prime suspect, the one they believed was responsible for the crime; they just didn't have enough evidence to act on that belief yet.

"Person of interest," I mused. "And just how did I acquire that designation?"

"Like I said, because you've been snooping around all over the school. Because you were seen leaving the victim's office last night. And because you were one of the last people to have spoken with a one Jason Fowler. And you've also been harassing people all over campus. Coaches, football players, parents, even the principal himself."

"Harassing?" I said, my voice starting to rise. "That's a stretch if I ever heard one. You actually think I had something to do with what happened here today? You have any proof of that beyond innuendo and whatever distorted info you've been fed?"

"We're the police, we don't need any proof right now," the average-looking detective said, and motioned to a squad car on the corner. "But you've got some explaining to do. Let's go do it down at the station house."

*

Pasadena police headquarters was located a block away from City Hall, across from a courthouse, with a firehouse down the street. The police station was merely one more government edifice, tucked away on a cul-de-sac where most residents ventured only when they needed to handle a traffic ticket. The room they led me into was small, poorly lit, and without windows. A lighting fixture holding a single naked bulb hung down from the ceiling. It felt like I had entered a 1940s noir movie. I wondered if there were any rubber hoses nearby to beat suspects who didn't cooperate.

The two detectives took turns interrogating me. The average-looking detective was named Al Diamond, and the short, stocky one was named Hugh Turco. They mostly asked the same questions in different ways; Diamond asked things in a bored, pro forma manner, while Turco acted like a sarcastic dork. Typical small-town police exercise, a variation of good cop-bad cop. They asked what type of soda I wanted, and when I told them a Coke, they brought me a can of ginger ale. Just to inform me who was running the show here. After an hour of relating the same story in the same way, I finally decided to give them something to chew on.

"You know," I said. "I really didn't want to be telling you this."

"Oh?" Turco said, his demeanor adding some interest. "What's that?"

"I used to be a cop. Just like you."

"I'm not a cop," he sneered.

"Oh, what are you then?"

"I'm a detective."

"Could have fooled me," I said.

Turco looked at me and went over to the corner. He picked up a telephone book. It was big and thick and looked like it was about 25 years old. Turco slapped it against his palm a few times.

"How'd you like to learn some manners?" he asked.

I was not in handcuffs, and figured I could disarm him and pummel him mercilessly if I chose to. Turco was smaller than me, didn't look especially tough, and I wouldn't have been surprised if the last fight he engaged in was during puberty. But I also was keenly aware that if I laid so much as a finger on him, it would not only lead to assault charges and jail time, but would unleash a cavalcade of police officers bursting into the room to stomp me.

"Look," I started, "it's been a long day for both of us. I apologize for my behavior. Maybe we can start fresh. But I've told you everything."

"Everything? I'm just learning now you used to be on the job."

"All right. Fair enough. You knew I was a licensed P.I. because I showed you my papers. And that I'm licensed to carry that gun you took off me earlier. I guess I figured you would have done a database search on me by now. The part about being on the job? I usually don't bring that up. Not every local police force is fond of LAPD. I didn't think it would help matters."

"Uh-huh. So you figured some small-town dipshits like us would resent a former big-city cop?"

"Something like that."

Turco shook his head and walked out of the room. He wisely took the phone book with him. No need to leave it here where I could pick it up and have it at the ready when he returned.

It took him about 45 minutes to come back, and this time he did so with Diamond in tow. The pair of them sat down across from me. Diamond continued to remind me of a cardboard cutout. Turco reminded me of a smarmy cop I used to work with named Andy Wax. The ongoing joke in the Broadway Division was that even Wax's best friends couldn't stand him.

"Now I know why you didn't tell me," said Turco, holding up a sheaf of papers.

"Yeah?"

"You were kicked off the force. I wouldn't be proud of that either."

"It's complicated," I said weakly.

"Sure. Says here that you were arrested for running a child prostitution ring. Those things are always complicated, aren't they?"

I swallowed hard. That happened almost ten years ago, and it was the worst period of my life. I had tried to help a teenage runaway start a better life, and I made a critical error in judgment. Judy Atkin was seventeen years old at the time I arrested her, but she looked thirteen, with the bluest eyes you ever saw. She had left Iowa to escape an abusive father, and when she arrived in Los Angeles, she fell into a situation that was actually worse. A pimp took her in, treated her nicely for a while, and then put her to work on the streets, threatening to kill her if she tried to leave. After we arrested the pimp and put him away for five years, Judy was still left with the problem of having no money and no home.

"I wasn't running anything," I said hotly.

"Your rap sheet says different."

"Does it say there that I wasn't convicted? That all charges were dropped?"

"Sure. But you know and I know, where there's smoke, there's fire."

"That's quite a leap."

"You were never fully exonerated, were you?"

What he was saying was technically true, but patently false. I had made the critical mistake of taking Judy in, giving her a place to live, albeit a temporary one. I wanted to give her the opportunity to get a fresh start on her own. She wouldn't go back to Des Moines, and I couldn't let her go back on the street. The only other option was placing her into the County's juvenile care system, and I had seen the devastating effects that had on kids. I tried to make a difference in her life, but turning tricks was what she knew. And when she began bringing johns into my apartment, my world came crashing down. She was scared, and the detectives who busted her said she accused me of being her pimp. I was carted unceremoniously off to jail, and the only reason I got off was because Judy skipped town and disappeared into the wind. With no witness, there was no case against me. Charges were dropped, but it was true, I did not get exonerated, only released. And my career in law enforcement spiraled downhill from there.

"That doesn't mean I was guilty. I wasn't."

"Yeah, they all say that, don't they? Come on. You were on the job. You must have heard every perp yapping about how they were innocent, huh?"

"Once in a while it's true," I managed.

"Sure. And you were a model policeman. L.A.'s finest."

"I was," I responded, ignoring the jibe. But after my arrest, I did become a changed cop. I used to be a by-the-book police officer. But after inhabiting a cell at the Twin Towers, sharing space with the same slime I had been locking up, my faith in the system disappeared.

"But that wasn't why you got kicked off the LAPD. Looks like you became a cowboy after that. Says here you were working plainclothes in North Hollywood. Some douche bag wouldn't cooperate, so you threw him into the trunk of your car for an hour. In ninety-one degree heat. That your idea of good police work?"

"No," I said. A small child had been kidnapped and the suspect fit the profile. By the time I yanked him out of the trunk, he was not only willing to tell me where the little boy was, but he took me right to him. And then he collapsed from heat exhaustion. The subsequent investigation did not paint my actions in a favorable light and I was written up. The first of a number of such reports. I had indeed gone rogue and it eventually cost me my job.

"You're a piece of work, Burnside."

"Tell me something I haven't heard," I said, starting to not care if he slapped me with a phone book. "But where are you going with this? All that stuff happened almost a decade ago."

"Yeah, and I'm just finding out about that now. You weren't so mouthy about your time on the job. What else are we going to find out here? That you knifed Jason Fowler because you had beef with him? That you put a shiv in his ribs because of some personal disagreement? Wouldn't surprise me. Everything with you seems to be personal."

"I never met him before yesterday. No way you can prove otherwise. And what possible motive could I have had?"

"You'd been on the St. Dismas campus before, right?"

"Only to talk to a couple of football players," I said. "And the coach. That was my only interest in the school."

"Yeah, that's what you keep saying. You used to be a recruiter. Recruiting kids. You're exceptionally good at that, huh?"

I took a deep breath and let it out. I decided it was a smarter move than telling Turco he was the equivalent of a fat piece of snot and too dumb to even get my drink order correct. But I wasn't going to get anywhere cracking wise. This was the fun part of a police detective's job, and as much as I wanted to throw Turco's pudgy body through a wall, I had no choice but to endure his taunts. These were the moments that small-time gnats like Turco lived for. They didn't have much else.

"I can't help you, Detective. I've told you everything I know about Jason Fowler."

"Okay. Sure. Then you wouldn't mind starting over again. From the beginning."

\*

It took another hour, but the Pasadena Police Department finally decided they didn't have any more questions and didn't have anything on which they could hold me. Turco's final admonishment to not leave town was met with a silent nod. My mouth stayed zipped. When I walked out of the police station, the sun was beginning to set, lighting up the distant San Gabriel Mountains with a purplish hue.

I looked at the traffic map on my iPhone, and all freeways leading out of Pasadena were solid red. There was also a Dodger game that was just starting, so passage through downtown would be jammed up for a while. I texted Gail that I missed her and Marcus but wouldn't be home for dinner. She texted back that I'd be missing her baked ziti and a Disney video.

I drove idly around Pasadena for a little while, looking for a place to eat. Over the years, the area had become home to a burgeoning Asian population, and there were now restaurants specializing in everything from Japanese ramen to Vietnamese pho to Taiwanese soup dumplings, and more. I was trying to decide if I was in the mood to experiment when I came upon a familiar site, an oddly named but remarkably good walk-up stand called The Hat. It had nothing to do with Asian cuisine. An old-school pastrami house, The Hat has been a landmark in the San Gabriel Valley for decades. I didn't think their pastrami was quite as good as at Langer's, the reigning king of pastrami purveyors in L.A. but this was a different style. The Hat served a pastrami dip, sliced very thin and stuffed into a roll. It was a little spicier and a little fattier than Langer's. The dip was similar to a French dip, in that the inside of the roll was briefly submerged into the juices in which the pastrami was cooked, making the sandwich soft and moist. Mustard and pickles were automatically added. It wasn't Langer's, but it wasn't bad at all. Just different. The pastrami was a tasty treat, but the prompt service at The Hat meant I only managed to shave 20 minutes off of my waiting-for-traffic-to-die-down time.

Since it would be a while before the freeways began flowing smoothly again, I decided to give my paying client a visit and provide him with an update. The benefit of going to Earl Bainbridge's estate was that I was able to view one of the most magnificent homes around. A huge, Tudor-style mansion, set on a hill above the Rose Bowl, it was spectacular in every way. From the stone fence to the carefully manicured grounds to the view of not only the Rose Bowl, but also the lush green grass of the Brookside golf course, this was simply a splendid property to behold. The downside to visiting the Bainbridge Estate, of course, was having to interact with Earl.

I parked my Pathfinder up the street and walked to the gate. Surprisingly, it was wide open, although I noticed what had to be a 50-year-old blue Ford Mustang warming up in the driveway, getting ready to depart. It was shiny and refurbished, and looked as if a lot of care had gone into it. The car backed up, but stopped abruptly as I darted out of its way. The driver's side window slid down.

"Hey, sorry about that," said a very large fellow, who, upon, further inspection, was actually a teenager.

"No problem. I always look both ways when I enter an estate like this. Say, that's quite a car. They don't make these anymore. It's a classic."

"Uh, yeah, I guess. It could use a brake job, they're starting to squeal. My dad got it a couple of years ago, he'd been restoring it. But he's been so busy at his restaurant. Actually I think it might be my mom's car now. I don't know. They split up."

"Sorry to hear that," I said.

"Yeah. It's been tough. He still comes by, but you know. It's hard. Say," he said, his voice now clearly resembling that of a kid more than a man. "Didn't I see you at practice yesterday?"

"Probably. I take it you're a football player."

"Yeah. You're a college scout, right?"

"Used to be," I said, getting a little tired of repeating the same old line. "I was coaching at SC for a few years. What's your name?"

"Dash Farsakian."

I nodded. "I guess you're friends with Austin."

"Sure. I've known Austin my whole life. We used to play touch football on the back lawn here. That was when Austin was going to be a quarterback in the NFL and I was going to be his tight end. Funny how things worked out. Now I'm a lineman."

"Well," I said, "not everything in life goes as planned."

"We're both listed as three-star players on the Internet sites. I don't know how that happened. I'd like to play college football somewhere. Always been my dream."

"Don't worry about those Internet sites," I said, dismissively. "Some of them are just amalgamators, they take other people's scouting reports and roll them together. I swear, a few of those sites are developed by people sitting in basements who've never even been to a high school football game. These people are about as qualified to evaluate football talent as a pastry chef."

Dash chuckled for a moment. "I guess."

"Look," I said, "when it comes to players, word gets around. And your program gets a lot of attention."

"Yeah. I'm grateful we have Noah. He's like a lightning rod. Feels like the whole world is watching us."

"They certainly were today," I observed.

"Oh," he said, finally recognizing the reference. "Yeah. Bad scene today at school. Couldn't believe it."

"Any thoughts on who might have been involved?" I asked as casually as I could.

Dash thought about this, opened his mouth for a moment and then closed it. "No. I really don't."

It didn't look like he wanted to talk anymore, so I reached into my pocket and handed him my business card. "If you think of anything, give me a buzz. Anything at all. You never know what might help."

"Uh, yeah. Sure," he said, pocketing my card and giving me a brief nod as he backed out quickly and drove up the hill.

I walked to the front door and, ignoring the doorbell, rapped on it. No one answered, so I wrapped harder. Finally, it opened. A tall, lanky teenager with dark brown hair layered with a bleached blond streak across the top opened the door.

"Hey. Can I help you?"

"Yes, my name's Burnside. Are you Austin?"

"I am."

"I'm actually here to see your dad. Is he taking visitors?"

Austin laughed. "That's funny. That's actually something Dad's friends might say. But no, he's not home. You might catch him over at the club."

"The club?"

"The Galley Hut Club. It's local. Mostly Pasadena people. Dad's usually there around now. Cocktail hour and all."

I laughed. It did strike me as odd that a person who owned a breathtaking estate like this needed to spend a lot of time somewhere else. Maybe he was bored. Or maybe he didn't appreciate what he had.

"Can you have your dad give me a call?" I asked and handed him my card. I'm sure Earl had my phone number, but people who traveled in Earl's circles often liked it when visitors left a calling card.

Austin looked down. "Oh. You're the guy Dad brought in to look into the fundraising scam at school."

"You know about that?" I asked.

"Sure. Dad told me he was hiring someone. Actually, I was the one who let on there were some funny things going on with the football program. Didn't need to push Dad too hard after that. He hates the coach. I'm not so happy with him, either."

"Uh-huh. I heard he replaced you at quarterback. I imagine that was tough."

"I guess. Hey, look, I've seen Noah throw the ball. I don't have his arm, but I'm pretty good, too. Just won't get the chance."

"You could have transferred," I pointed out.

"Nah. St. Dismas is five minutes away. And Dad would have sent me to Eastridge, otherwise. That's where he went. Same as my grandfather."

"Got it."

"So what's going on with the fundraising? You catch who did it?"

"Not yet," I said. "Who do you think did it?"

"Hey, I only know Dad wrote a large check to the school and the money's not being spent. No one's talking. Coach told Dad to mind his own business when he asked about it. You can imagine how well that went over."

Knowing Earl Bainbridge, I could imagine indeed. And that was why I was hanging out in blistering Pasadena the past two days. I was discovering things, but not much about fundraising.

"So let me ask you something, Austin. That incident at school today. With Jason Fowler. What do you make of it?"

Austin cocked his head for a long minute in mock thought. It was a nice pose, but it was as fake as a three dollar bill. "Mr. Fowler seemed like a nice guy. But he really wasn't. He took advantage of situations."

"What do you mean?"

"I can't really talk about it. Other than to say I wasn't surprised."

"Well, now you've got my attention."

He smiled. "Look, I don't mean anything by it. I don't know who did it, I really don't."

I took a chance. "Rumor had it he was sexually involved with one of the girls."

He stared at me. "I ... didn't know that," he said. "Which girls?"

"Not sure," I said. "I'm only going on scuttlebutt."

"What's scuttlebutt?"

"Gossip. Nothing substantive."

At that point, a shiny white Mercedes pulled into the driveway. An attractive blonde woman in her early 30s got out, walking in an unsteady way. She was dressed stylishly, fitting neatly into a tight, little black cocktail dress. She looked mildly drunk.

"Hi, Austin," she smiled, her white teeth glistening. "Who's your cute friend?"

"Oh, hi there, Mitzi. This is Mr. Burnside. He's a detective Dad hired."

"A detective?" she said, the smile vanishing from her face.

"It's okay. Dad's not doing another marital investigation. Someone else pissed him off. You're in the clear."

"That's rude, Austin." she said and turned toward me, holding out her hand for me to shake. "I'm Melissa Bainbridge. Sorry we didn't get introduced appropriately."

"No problem," I said, reaching over and briefly grasping her hand in a polite-yet-distant manner. "I'm just leaving. I was here to see Earl, but it looks like I'll miss him."

"He's working on his third gin and tonic, so yes, it may be a while."

I smiled. "Funny, I had Earl pegged as a martini guy."

Austin laughed. "I don't know how people drink those things. Give me a beer any day."

Melissa gave him a look. "I don't think your father would like hearing that."

"Coo coo ca choo," he mumbled.

I took a breath and tried to figure out if it was better to stay or leave. Sometimes an interesting tidbit spilled out. Sometimes staying was a waste of time. But hanging around also meant getting seeped in another family's dirty water. Knowing Earl Bainbridge's history of multiple marriages and divorces, there was only so much I wanted to get exposed to.

"You'll tell Earl I stopped by?" I asked, looking back and forth at the two of them.

"Sure," Austin said. "And about that other thing?"

"Yes?"

"I think Mr. Fowler had it coming to him," Austin said, glancing at his stepmother before looking back at me. "At least that's what a few of the guys on the team are saying."

# *Five*

The Dodgers were in the 4th inning of their game with the Cardinals at Chavez Ravine, finally enabling me to sail easily through downtown. The absence of traffic also allowed me to catch glimpses of the sparkling high-rises that had sprung up on either side of the Harbor Freeway. Not long ago, downtown L.A. consisted mostly of a small cluster of skyscrapers surrounded by a large swath of poverty. Raging development had led to the construction of countless office towers and slick condos in the area, although pockets of poor neighborhoods still remained, intertwined with the soaring growth.

The temperature had cooled off as I pulled into our driveway in Mar Vista, the evening air of the Westside offering a break from the sizzling temperatures of Pasadena. In some parts of the country, the hot weather lingers continuously in the summer, regardless of whether it's day or night. But In L.A., the sun going down is normally a sure sign that the heat will abate soon.

Our house was eerily quiet even though it was only 8:30 p.m. A child in the home means frequent noise, at least in our household, and the absence of such typically indicates the child has gone to bed. I walked into my office and immediately took my brand new .357 pistol out of the ankle holster and stowed it away in the safe. I used an ankle holster in the summer because, without a jacket, there was no other way to hide my gun. Openly carrying a pistol was illegal in California, and worse, it made people uncomfortable to see an armed man casually walking around in public.

I strolled into the kitchen and the whiff of garlic gave me a reminder of the remnants of dinner. A pan on the stove held some tube-style pasta, sausage, and marinara sauce. But with the pastrami dip from The Hat still lingering deep in my stomach, there would be no room for any more culinary delights tonight.

"Hi there."

I turned and saw Gail, her hair falling past her shoulders, wearing sweats, makeup off, but still looking extraordinarily pretty. I went over and gave her a hug. She hugged me back.

"I'm sorry," I said.

"For what?"

"For whatever. Any transgressions past or present. Or future."

She gave a small smile. If there was one more thing I loved about Gail, she just didn't hold grudges. Disagreements were treated like tissue paper, used and then discarded.

"All right," she said and gave me a kiss. "I'm lucky in one respect."

"How so?"

"With you and Marcus, I only have to live with two men. Snow White had to live with seven."

I laughed. "I guess I know what movie you two watched tonight. Maybe *The Lion King* would have been a better choice for him."

"Or for you."

"Perhaps. Speaking of which, I assume our little guy conked out early?" I asked. Seeing Marcus when I came home made my day. Hearing him trumpet my arrival was better than having the P.A. announcer shout my name to 90,000 fans as I ran onto the Coliseum floor when I played for USC. Marcus was the validation that I had fully become an adult, a parent with responsibilities. I didn't have a dad growing up, mine died before I was born. So the fact that I could become a father myself was a very big deal for me. But it also meant I had no role model for being a dad, and it sometimes felt as if I were operating in the dark.

"Yes, Marcus didn't even make it to the end of the movie. He was tired. They run them pretty ragged at that pre-school."

"I figured as much," I said with a sigh. "Any more bumper tag issues?"

"No," Gail said. "And it looks like Marcus and Ricky are becoming friends. All it took was a scuffle."

"Boys," I smiled. "Part of the bonding process. Starts at a young age."

"So I'm learning. How are you holding up?" Gail asked, stroking my arm. "I heard about what happened at St. Dismas this morning. It was all over the news."

"I was in the school building when it happened."

"Oh, my. How close?"

"I was with the principal when the body was discovered, but it could have happened hours before. Coincidentally, I was talking with that teacher last night. "

"That's strange."

"Indeed. And the Pasadena Police were a tad skeptical of my story. And of me as well. One of them got a hold of the Judy Atkin file and decided to rake me over the coals with it."

"Ouch. Sorry you have to keep reliving that."

"It's a part of my history, for better or worse. As long as I'm in this field, someone is going to bring it up. It's funny how your past never quite lets go of you."

"That's what psychologists say."

I smiled. One of the items on my to-do list was to speak further with Noah Greenland's mother. I had the feeling she would be analyzing me as much as I'd be assessing her.

"Hopefully I won't need to be on some psychologist's couch any time soon," I said. "If I have any head issues, they're probably related to a concussion or two from back in the day."

"I guess that's hard to avoid, having played football," she winced. "And it's a big concern I have with Marcus. He idolizes you. I could see him wanting to follow in your footsteps."

"Is that bad?"

"No, sweetie. But Marcus is so bright. I don't want to risk things like head injuries. Do you know what I mean?"

"I do," I said. "We have a lot of years ahead of us before this needs addressing."

"Yes," Gail said, and then her head perked up. "Oh. I just remembered. Speaking of someone in need of psychotherapy, you got a call tonight. From that wacky neighbor of ours in Santa Monica. The woman who lived downstairs. The one with the, er, loud lifestyle."

"Ms. Linzmeier?" I frowned.

"Right. She told me she tried to reach you on your cell, but it went straight to voice mail. Said it was urgent. I didn't know you had taken her on as a client."

While I normally told Gail about all of my cases, I hadn't quite gotten around to looping her in on this one, our tiff last night taking precedence over candid conversations.

"I had my cell phone turned off when I was in the police station. Didn't think it would go over well to take client calls while they were grilling me about a homicide. But I never gave her our home phone number. I'm a little concerned she could access it. I had our address and phone numbers wiped from most of the internet sites."

Gail sighed. "Maybe the apartment manager gave it to her."

"I guess. Ms. Linzmeier showed up in my office yesterday. Thinks her boyfriend is cheating, wants me to look into it. My favorite type of case."

"Yuk. Not much good comes from those things. I'm sure you suggested she confront him about it."

"Yeah, but she doesn't trust her boyfriend to tell her the truth. Wouldn't believe him if he told her he was being faithful. Anyway, I said I'd help her. Shouldn't take much time. Let me give her a call now. If I don't, she's the type who'll call back at midnight and wake Marcus up."

Gail kissed my cheek. "Some people have no boundaries."

"She's just nervous," I said and walked into the den. I pulled out my phone and found her number. My long day was unending. She answered on the first ring.

"Burnside. Thanks for calling. Listen, I have some information. It's all set. Doug told me he's got a business dinner tomorrow at Shutters. He had the same expression on his face, just like before. Wouldn't look me in the eye. He's hiding something, I know it, I just know it. It's so obvious. We need to catch him in the act. I am so ... "

"Okay, okay," I said, trying to mask my exasperation. "I get it."

"So you'll do the sting tomorrow?"

"It's not a sting, Rebecca. It's a stakeout. I'll be there and I'll find out what he's doing."

"Okay. Let me know where you'll be."

I took a deep breath. This was the worst of all scenarios. If someone catches their partner cheating on them, it can only lead to bad things. There are no upsides to this type of confrontation. I calculated what I was going to charge her and realized that no matter how high I upped my rate, it would never be enough to compensate for the pain and suffering, which is to say, my own.

"That won't work," I told her. "At all. You can't be there. Non-negotiable. In fact, unless you promise me right now that you won't show up, I'm pulling out of this."

"I can't even see for myself?"

"Absolutely not. Do you trust me to tell you the truth?"

A long moment ensued. "Yes," she said quietly.

I waited a moment before I asked the next question. This was the most critical of all. Because as much as someone wants to know whether their partner is engaging in illicit activities, a certain side of them might actually prefer to remain in the dark.

"Do you want to know the truth?" I asked. "Are you sure you're ready for it? Really sure?"

"I don't know," she said, and I thought I heard the slightest hint of a sniffle. "I suppose I'll have to be."

*

The jets at Santa Monica Airport began warming up at 5:00 a.m. Our next-door neighbor told us that at one time there was a generally accepted rule that, apart from dire emergencies, planes did not take off or land before 6:30 a.m. or after 10:30 p.m. That rule, like many others in our society, has eroded, as the personal needs of some overwhelmed the slightest hint of consideration for anyone else.

I made a pot of French roast and began my day. Earl Bainbridge had sent me a text at 2:00 a.m. saying he wanted to speak with me, but he also indicated he'd be going to sleep soon. I made a mental note to call him around lunchtime. I combed the Internet and read through the stories about St. Dismas and Jason Fowler, which had indeed become national news. Teacher slain by a knife-wielding killer, no suspects, but vague mentions of an outside intruder possibly involved. Police had no leads, although they were speaking with certain individuals who were in the building at the time, ones who had no business being on campus. Fortunately, no names were given, and there was no leak that might indicate a certain private investigator's presence at the scene.

Marcus was up early, quietly sauntering into the office and climbing into my lap. I quickly minimized the news pages and brought up the Nickelodeon site. I handed him the mouse and allowed him to surf the Internet, which meant he was clicking on anything that was colorful and flashing. The upside was it allowed him to satisfy his insatiable curiosity. The downside was my computer might get a virus. Somehow he burrowed a trail to the Playboy en *Español* site, and I needed to show him that computers had a back button. I helped him navigate to an online coloring book that was more age appropriate, and we spent some quality time re-painting the Mona Lisa into vivid shades of purple, red and green.

Once Gail was dressed and cooking breakfast, I headed out to beat traffic up to Pasadena. I found another Starbucks, this one on Lake Avenue, and continued my online perusing over more coffee and a lemon scone. The *Pasadena Star-News* featured the Jason Fowler story in depth, although their article focused more on the school's storied history and went into greater detail about the now fragile state of the students and faculty.

At about 8:30 a.m., I decided classes had probably started at St. Dismas, and I might be able to continue whatever mottled investigation I was conducting. What started out as misappropriation of funds had morphed into homicide. While I didn't think the two were related, it was still coincidental that Jason Fowler was murdered less than a day after I spoke with him.

I pulled open the front door and approached yet another new security guard. But instead of getting a warm, lazy greeting, I was met with a grim-faced block of granite. He approached me with an outstretched arm, a motion that communicated I needed to stop in my tracks.

"Please state your business," he said curtly.

"I'm here to see Coach Savich."

"Do you have an appointment?"

"He's expecting me," I said, the fingers starting to cross on my hand.

"I need to see some I.D."

I handed him my driver's license and watched him paw over it, looking up at me and then down at the license twice. Then he picked up a phone and punched in a few numbers. After 30 seconds of nothing, he left a brief message and hung up.

"Looks like Coach Savich isn't around."

"Maybe I can wait in his office."

"Sorry, but we can't allow that. Not after what happened yesterday."

"I understand," I said. "Okay if I wait here until he comes for me?"

The security officer mulled this over for a minute before finally shrugging and pointing to a beige metal folding chair with a number of deep scratches on the seat. I whittled away the time, putting together my all-time list of the top ten USC running backs. I had secured most of the slots when a familiar body lumbered past. I almost felt a shadow wash over me.

"Oh my. We're blessed with the presence of a USC Trojan," said Curly Underwood. He motioned to the security guard that everything was all right.

"Coach," I said, standing up and extending a hand. He reached over and grabbed it, and it felt like I was shaking hands with a hunk of tri-tip.

"Strong grip," I said. "I'll bet no one bullied you out of your lunch money when you were a kid."

"Nope. You Trojans need to work out more," he laughed and motioned for me to follow him. We walked down the hall together, and it resembled a person walking alongside a moving tree.

"So I'm sensing a bit of hostility toward SC," I remarked.

"Maybe a little."

"Anything I've done? I mean, besides insult your nickname."

"I'll get over it, I've been dealing with that nickname my whole life. No, I got nothing against you personally. But we had a player last year that was offered a scholarship to your school. Demarco Ferguson. Good tight end. He wanted to go there, too, Lord only knows why. But it turned out Cleary managed to sign a couple of blue-chip tight ends after that. So SC pulled the offer. Kid's playing at Colorado State. Not a bad school, but it's not what he had his heart set on."

This was not an uncommon story. USC, like most top-tier college programs, offered a lot of kids scholarships. Not all of them would accept. We had only 25 scholarships a year to dispense, and needed to parse them out in the way that was best for the team's future. If we offered five tight ends, maybe one or two might accept and we'd take both of them. In this case, there was one too many tight ends who wanted to come aboard. And when that happens, tough decisions need to be made. In some cases, we delayed admission for a semester, something called a gray shirt, meaning the kid's scholarship would count toward the following year's class. But in other cases, keeping the offer just wasn't workable, and disappointment, or in this case, lingering hostility on the part of the high school coaches, was the result.

"Sorry about that," I said. "Recruiting is sometimes a numbers game."

"That what you told Demarco?" he asked sarcastically.

"I don't know. But it does work both ways. Some kids pop quickly and commit to one school, but then at the last minute, they change their minds and switch. So the college is left scrambling to fill a hole."

"Mmm-hmmm."

"So how's preparation for De La Salle coming? Tomorrow night's a big game. Eyes of the nation will be on you."

"I'm well aware. But we didn't need all that drama yesterday. I couldn't believe there were guys from CNN on campus."

I took a breath. "A murder at a high school is big news."

"Yeah, sure. But it's also a big distraction. We need to get these kids ready to play."

I didn't quite know how to respond to such deep sensitivity, so I didn't say anything. I wanted to ask Underwood about the fundraising issues, but sensed I should first talk to Savich. No sense poisoning the well just yet. We reached the athletic offices, and sure enough Coach Savich wasn't there.

"You can have a seat," Underwood said. "I'll go find Duke. He can't be too far."

I sat down in the small office, which wasn't much bigger than a cubbyhole and smelled distinctly of sweaty socks and body odor. Scattered about the office was some knockabout furniture, which might have been procured from a garage sale. A far cry from Principal Mularkey's plush office, Savich's had a small desk piled high with files, and an assortment of photos and Notre Dame memorabilia. I looked out the window and saw one of the equipment managers sitting on the grass, working at removing mud that had caked up inside some of the cleats. A pile of athletic shoes sat next to him.

"Well, looky here. The pride of USC. Or former pride I should say," boomed Duke Savich as he strolled into his office. I thought of getting up to shake his hand, but something about his tone kept me planted in my seat.

"You guys really have a thing about SC. Underwood told me one of your kids had an offer pulled last year. Wasn't personal. Wasn't my doing either."

"Nah," he said. "That ain't it. I just don't like you Toejams. My Fighting Irish background and all."

"You take this stuff too seriously," I said, glad I hadn't brought along any doughnuts, and trying to hold back a few observations about his maturity.

"Everyone needs a hobby."

"Yeah, right," I said dryly. "Look, Coach, I only came here to ask you a few questions. On behalf of a parent."

"Yeah, yeah. I heard from Mularkey. Old Earl has his panties in a bunch again. He's been ticked at us since we gave the QB slot to Noah and pushed Austin to receiver. Earl always needs something to rail about."

"So the principal talked with you," I said slowly.

"Yeah. And even if this were any of Earl's business -- which it isn't -- I'm not about to share confidential information with some half-assed gumshoe who's been wandering around the school unimpeded."

"Meaning?" I peered at him, wondering how he knew the definition of unimpeded, and thinking I'd like to throw an unimpeded left hook into his big mouth.

"Meaning I'd be curious to know where you were when Jason Fowler was killed."

"I'll tell you the same thing I told the police," I said, beginning to fume. "I was with Principal Mularkey."

"That's just when they found the body. Fowler had been knifed earlier in the morning," Savich sneered.

"Funny, you seem to know a lot about the facts of this case. I'd be curious where *you* were yesterday morning. Sharpening your switchblade?"

Savich pointed a finger at me. "I'm warning you. Don't start anything. You don't know what kind of guy I am. I have a short fuse with people that mess with me."

"And I know all about guys like you," I said evenly. "Guys who wear the same socks every day when their favorite team is on a winning streak. Guys who think it's cool to wear a football jersey when they take a girl out on a first date. Guys who think it's okay to bust someone's chops just because they think they can."

"You've got a real big mouth," he said, taking a step toward me.

"Sure I do. And I'll bet you have big spending habits. You gamble the fundraising money away? Or just steal it outright and wire the money to an offshore account."

"You're making some nasty charges, you prick."

"And I'm making them to a very small man."

"I'm warning you," he snarled, taking another step, his breathing starting to deepen like a rhino building steam. "Shut your trap."

"You already warned me. Did you forget already?"

"Maybe you got a hearing problem."

"Maybe you have a speaking problem."

"Oh, you're really asking for it," he said, the slightest of smiles forming on his face.

"Am I? I'll bet Notre Dame wait-listed you before you got accepted. I guess they have different admission standards for the local South Bend kids. Which is most likely, none at all."

And with that, his eyes bulging out and his nostrils flaring, Duke Savich reared back and threw an overhand right at my head. I knew it was coming and raised my left arm high to block it. I drove my right fist deep into his stomach and heard the air go out of him. I let go of his right arm and slammed my left fist into the right side of his face. He crumpled over and went down on one knee. Proper ring etiquette might have been for me to step back and wait for him to catch his breath. But people like Duke Savich would demonstrate their appreciation by getting up and taking another swing at my head. I did take a step back, but only to line up and deliver a nasty kick to the left side of his face. He went sprawling onto the ground and let out a yelp. Apparently it was loud enough to draw attention, the type of which was not what I wanted.

It took about five seconds for Curly Underwood to come racing in. Seeing Savich on the ground holding his head, he turned to me.

"This is what you came here to do?" he demanded.

"No," I said, continuing to step back. "Things, um, got a little out of hand."

"I'm going to escort you out," he said, grabbing my left arm and yanking me toward the door. I jerked my arm back and instinctively reached down into my ankle holster. Out came my .357 Magnum. I put my hands together in case Underwood decided to try and grab it. He was certainly strong enough to pull it out of my hand, but not when I had both hands wrapped tightly around it. At least not until I had time to pull the trigger.

"Step back," I ordered. "Now. I mean it."

Underwood raised his hands in a defensive posture and started moving away from me. "Hold on there, cowboy. Take it easy now."

I pointed to a chair and told him to sit down. He sat. I locked the office door and we waited for Duke Savich to gather what was left of his wits and pull himself up to a kneeling position. You could practically see little blue jays flying around his head, chirping merrily. It took almost three minutes before he was composed enough to speak. It wasn't worth the wait.

"You fucking prick," he managed hoarsely.

"That's not very nice," I said and briefly debated whether to use the butt end of the .357 to smack him again. Had Underwood not been sitting there waiting for an opening, I might have been tempted.

"Uh-huh," he managed.

"Let's start by you answering some questions," I said.

"Get lost," he responded.

"Hey. I'm the one holding the gun. I'm the one that gets to deliver the insults," I told him. "And if either of you decides to get brave and take a run at me, I'm shooting both of you."

Underwood and Savich eyed each other nervously, as if they had been reading each other's minds. Savich finally shook his head. "Look, I don't know how we can help you."

Surveying the scene, I briefly considered how I arrived at this peculiar moment. At the start of the week, I was merely planning to do a simple investigation for a cranky client. Now I was in the unenviable situation of trying to squeeze the details of fundraising discrepancies out of two high school football coaches at gunpoint. Unfathomable, perhaps. But here I was.

"Tell me why Earl Bainbridge hired me," I said.

Savich sighed. "It's complicated."

"So's having a .357 pointed at you."

"Hey. There are some things that are confidential. You know and I know you're not going to shoot us."

I knew that, too. But sometimes a bluff can be worth it. "If I shoot one of you, I'll have to shoot and kill both of you. No witnesses. You attacked me, my life was endangered and I defended myself. Open and shut case."

They stared at me. "You're joking," Savich said.

"I wouldn't push that. You're the one who attacked me in the first place. All because you couldn't handle a couple of insults."

"I don't like you," he said.

"I don't like you, either. But that doesn't mean I get to act on every feeling."

"Look," Savich said, his voice starting to get annoyed. "There's no stealing going on here. I'm not getting rich off of this, I can assure you."

"Someone is," I pointed out. "Unless you think over a hundred grand isn't a lot of money."

Underwood shook his head. "This is L.A. Maybe it's not."

"Okay. Let's say I believe you're not stealing. I'll pretend for a minute the money is going to a worthy cause," I said and stopped for a moment and listened to my own words. "Or maybe not so worthy. But I'll assume for a minute it's not going into your pocket. What is the big secret then?"

"If word gets out," Savich insisted, "we have a lot of problems with a lot of people. We'd get smeared, so would a few others. And the money? It's not going anywhere evil. That I can assure you."

I shook my head and looked at the pair. A gun pointed at them, veiled threats, and they still weren't going to talk. I decided to try a different tack. "How is this tied to what happened yesterday? The murder of Jason Fowler."

"I don't know that it is," Savich said. "Fowler had nothing to do with the football team. It's unrelated."

A loud knock came on the door. "Hey, Coach?"

The two of them suddenly looked up at me in unison. I put my index finger to my lips and lowered my voice. "Not a word about any of this," I whispered in my most threatening voice, which may not have come off as all that threatening, but when you have a gun in your hand, people tend to pay attention. I had no intention of shooting them, but threats can work wonders on behavior. "You hear me? I can come back, you know."

They both nodded quickly. A little too quickly perhaps, but I didn't have much of a choice. There was now another person potentially involved, and I wasn't about to keep them all hostage. I holstered my weapon and stepped back. I motioned to Savich to go over and open the door, which he did, although he was walking unevenly.

"Hi, Coach," said the equipment manager, a kid who looked as if he were barely sixteen. "I'm almost done with the cleats. But I have Biology in a few minutes. Can I finish up later?"

"Sure," said Savich.

The manager walked off. Without looking at Savich and Underwood, I left the office and trailed him down the hallway. I shot a glance behind us, and we weren't being followed. Nevertheless I quickened my pace.

"What's your name," I asked.

"Colin. Colin Holder."

"You're the team manager?"

"Equipment manager, mostly. You?"

"Interested observer," I said and flashed my fake gold shield. This was a plastic imitation of a police detective's badge which spelled out "Private Investigator" in navy blue lettering, in front of a design resembling a sunburst. Most people never got close enough to read it, nor were they able to easily do so in the one solitary second in which I presented it for viewing. But in that one second, I got their attention, and even though I wasn't a part of any legitimate police department, the badge evoked the very clear impression that I was.

"Oh, wow," he said, his eyes widening.

"What were you doing out there?"

"Just cleaning dirt out of the cleats, sir."

"I was wondering about that. You usually don't see dirt trapped in cleats unless it's muddy. We haven't had rain here in six months."

"I know. Big drought. They need to get field turf. The practice field is weird here. It's always wet."

I frowned. "Seen anything else strange around here lately? Maybe related to what happened yesterday?"

He looked at me in a different way. "What do you mean?"

"Know anyone who'd like to harm Mr. Fowler?"

He didn't answer right away. We continued to walk.

"It's okay," I said. "You can talk freely. Better to speak what you know."

"Mr. Fowler," Colin finally said. "He's been pretty friendly with some of the girls. I've seen them talking together. Real close like, you know? I thought the whole thing was retarded."

"Which girls?"

"I don't really know. I didn't get a good look."

"A good look at what? Just what do you mean?"

He stopped and glared at me. "I mean, I heard Mr. Fowler screwing someone last night. In some office. Mrs. Swain's office, I think. It was late, well after practice. Like, right on top of a desk. They were going at it pretty good. I didn't get a look at them, the blinds were drawn. I walked away pretty quick. Didn't feel it was my place to stare."

"Did you tell the police this?"

"There's nothing to tell, man. Like I said. I didn't see who the girl was."

## *Six*

Climbing quickly into my Pathfinder, I turned over the ignition and roared away from St. Dismas. No one was behind me, so after about fifteen blocks, I pulled over onto a side street and began to ponder what to do next. There was still some coffee in my Starbucks cup, and I lifted it up and took a sip. Under the glow of an unyielding Pasadena sun, it had remained warm and curiously soothing. I thought of returning and getting a refill. I thought of going back to the police and telling them about my conversation with Colin Holder. I thought about driving to the beach and going for a swim. Instead, I took out my iPad and looked up an address. Fortunately, her office wasn't very far. Nothing in Pasadena was very far.

Dr. Stacy Greenland's practice was located off Colorado Boulevard, a few blocks from Old Town. There were some open meters on the street, but they all had one-hour time limits and I didn't know how long I'd be. I also didn't like the idea of having my Pathfinder in public view, considering I had just brandished a weapon and effectively held two men hostage for a few minutes, something the Pasadena police would likely take a dim view of if they got wind of it. Instead, I parked around the corner in an enclosed garage that advertised all-day parking for $10. I might be with the doctor for just a few minutes, but I might well be there longer. Turning into the garage, I handed the money to a bored looking man standing inside a kiosk, who pointed toward some open spaces in the back.

Her office was in a stylish, nine-story Art Deco building, the exterior painted in various shades of gray, with burgundy accents. The interior was much the same. I scanned through the directory and saw that most of the tenants were medical or therapeutic professionals, podiatrists, chiropractors, or psychologists and the like. There was even a listing for an organization that called itself The Tranquility Center. Out of curiosity, I walked by their office, only to see a hastily posted sign in blue magic marker that indicated the occupants had been evicted for nonpayment of rent.

I took the elevator up to the fourth floor and found Dr. Greenland's office, the sign on the door detailing that her practice did marriage, family, and child counseling. I entered the waiting room and sat down on a plush, comfy chair. It was a quarter to ten, and a few minutes later, a dour looking middle-aged couple walked in. Neither said hello or acknowledged my presence. The man clearly looked like he'd rather be elsewhere. The woman walked across the room and pushed a button, which turned on a small yellow light. At 10:00 a.m., Stacy Greenland opened the door, turned off the yellow light, and invited them inside. She frowned as she took note of me.

"May I help you?" she asked.

"Yes. The name is Burnside. We spoke briefly yesterday."

"I remember. What are you doing here?"

"I was hoping for a few minutes of your time."

"I'm sorry. I have patients all morning."

"I can wait," I said, well aware that I didn't have a lot else planned today.

She looked at me pensively. "I can give you a few minutes at noon. But I would prefer it if you didn't wait here," she said, and closed the door without bothering to inquire if that was all right with me.

Dr. Greenland may not have preferred it, but I chose to sit in her waiting room anyway. One never knows who one might meet. As it turned out, the only other patient was a sad-eyed young woman who arrived just before her 11:00 a.m. appointment. I spent two hours reading through the magazines Dr. Greenland subscribed to. *The Atlantic* and *Architectural Digest* were interesting, *U.S. News & World Report* and *Psychology Today* were not. I was debating whether to suggest she subscribe to *Sports Illustrated*, when the door opened and the Doctor ushered me in. I hadn't noticed the other patients leaving, so I assumed there was a special exit for them, or perhaps a trap door that sent them directly to the ground floor.

"Well, Mr. Burnside, what is it you wish to speak with me about?" she asked. She didn't sit and didn't invite me to do so either.

"I'm doing an investigation of the fundraising at St. Dismas. I'm talking to a number of people. Teachers, coaches, parents, kids. Anyone who might be able to shine a light on what's going on there."

"And just what do you think *is* going on there?" she asked.

"A lot of the money that was raised for the team has apparently disappeared. Unaccounted for. One of the parents is concerned."

"Oh. Well, I don't know how I can help you. We're not in a position to donate."

I looked around Dr. Greenland's spacious office. There was some original artwork on the walls, an antique walnut desk in the corner and a pair of expensive-looking black leather recliners facing each other. Stationed nearby was what looked like a psychologist's couch. It wasn't exactly a couch, but more akin to an elongated chair that allowed patients to lie in a supine position, relax, and share their deepest, darkest thoughts. It looked comfortable and I wondered how many patients had fallen asleep on it.

"I understand Noah is on scholarship."

"Yes, the school has been very generous."

I looked at her and said nothing. My experience with psychotherapists had been limited to a few instances, back in my LAPD days, when I had been involved in a shooting and the department mandated a number of sessions. The therapists I saw were very good at eliciting conversation by saying little, if anything. And while these therapists weren't trying to pass their techniques on to me, I eventually incorporated some of their tactics. They often worked on suspects, and they were now working on Stacy Greenland.

"You know," she finally said, a little wearily, "I wasn't crazy about Noah's going there, and I'm still not crazy about Noah playing football. I'm very worried about concussions."

Her concern was not unfounded, and the sport was taking some steps to remedy this, making changes to try and protect the players. I got the feeling that in a few decades, the game of football might be played very differently from the way it is today.

"That's interesting," I commented. "Has Noah had any concussion issues?"

"No, fortunately not yet. But every time he gets hit on the field, I think I die a little."

"That's a tough one," I said. "If you get this upset, why did you even let Noah go out for football? There are other sports he probably could have played. Baseball can always use pitchers with good arms."

Her mouth tightened. "Noah insisted. Make that demanded. I let him play flag football when he was in middle school, but I refused to let him play tackle football. These coaches all saw what a great arm he had and were recruiting him. Bob wanted him to play. My husband. He's totally seeped in the sport."

"Of course," I said and then started being exceptionally nosy. "He's a football coach. Wasn't he a coach when you got married?"

She stiffened. "He was a teacher. Bob didn't become a coach until later. But you don't choose who you fall in love with. It chooses you."

I thought about that for a moment and decided to move

on before I got a headache. "So you didn't let Noah play at first."

"No. I put my foot down. We enrolled him in the local public high school. Bob didn't like it, Noah didn't like it. He wasn't making friends. And then after his freshman year, Duke Savich offered him a scholarship to St. Dismas. I wouldn't budge. So Noah shut down on me."

"Shut down?"

"Yes, he shut down. Went on a speaking strike. He froze me out. Wouldn't talk to me all summer. And then when school began, he wouldn't get out of bed. Wouldn't go to school. Our house became one big battle zone. Noah felt I was manipulating him, not letting him have the life he wanted. I was only trying to protect him."

"So you relented."

"Yes," she said, shaking her head. "I had to. I was losing my son. We couldn't go on the way we were. Something had to give. As a parent, you don't have as much power as you think you do. I've reconciled with it. He gets to go to a good school for free."

"And so you enrolled him at St. Dismas."

"Yes. Noah was happy. At least at first. Then he started to recognize all the pressure that was on him. He had to win every week, or else he would shoulder the blame for losing."

I sighed. It's an issue with the quarterback position. They get too much credit when the team wins and too much grief when the team loses. Quarterback is the most important factor in a team's success, but it's still a team game. And people watching from the stands won't recognize when a play gets botched because a receiver runs the wrong route, or when a lineman fails to make a key block. Fans just see a quarterback throwing what looks like a bad pass that gets intercepted. And it's easy to label someone a failure, even when the outcome of a game is not their fault.

"So is your husband still involved in football?" I asked.

"Yes. He runs a clinic for elite quarterbacks now."

"Probably a lot of demand."

"Maybe. I don't know. There are a lot of people doing that sort of thing. He'd like to get back into coaching at a school. Start getting a regular paycheck and put us onto a decent health insurance plan."

"I didn't think things would be so tough for a doctor," I said.

"My practice is down, but we're managing," she said. "But what is this about fundraising? That's what you came to talk about. I apologize. Every time I think of Noah and football, I get sidetracked."

"I'm sorry about what you're going through. But regarding fundraising, something's going on at the school, and no one's talking. I'm asking questions and getting nowhere. I figure the more people I speak with, maybe someone can provide some insight."

"I see."

I tried another tack. "Are you friendly with Dash's mother? Skye Farsakian?"

"I know her, of course. She's the team parent. She does a lot of the organizing. She has the time."

"What do you mean she has the time?"

"Oh, nothing," Stacy Greenland said with a wave of her hand. "Skye's been a stay-at-home mom. She doesn't work outside the house. Or at least up until now. Her husband owns a restaurant in town, the Valley Steakhouse. It was popular for a while, but I guess it hasn't been doing so well lately. I heard he had to reduce staff and give his employees a pay cut."

"I imagine that didn't go over well," I said.

"I wouldn't know. But Wally moved out, took up with a younger woman, a waitress, I'm sure you're familiar with that type of story. You can only imagine how devastated Skye was. Poor thing. But I heard the girl dumped Wally, so he's trying to get back together with Skye. If she'll take him back, that is. I sure wouldn't."

I listened quietly, although I didn't quite know what to do with this. "I'm sure that's been rough on her."

"Yes. She's not quite the same person these days. It's hard to be ... abandoned like that."

"How so?" I asked.

"That should be obvious, Mr. Burnside."

It was, but it never hurts to ask, I thought. "You think she has a lot of anger?"

"Of course. I mean, we all do."

"Are you and Skye close?"

"Not really," she responded, oddly looking past me. "But our boys are friendly and they play on the team. She's not my type of person, she only has a high school degree, so there's limits to what we can talk about. But when you have children, you tend to associate more with the parents of the friends they make. For better or worse."

"All right," I said, an involuntary sigh coming out of me. "Thank you for taking a few minutes to speak with me. Would you mind if I talked with your husband?"

She paused for a moment. "I suppose, but he's traveling today. He'll be at the game tomorrow night. I'm sure you can catch him there. Although you'll probably have to fight your way through a dozen college recruiters. They always manage to surround us."

I didn't bother to tell her I was pretty good at fighting my way through a lot of things. As I turned to leave I asked her a final question. "Where do you think Noah will wind up? College, I mean."

"Stanford wants him," she said crisply, and I thought I saw a hint of exasperation cross her face. "I'm pushing him to go there. A full scholarship to Stanford would be phenomenal. But Bob wants to explore other options. I gather Stanford recruited another top quarterback last year, and he's already the starter. Bob thinks Noah can play in the NFL and make a lot of money, but it means going to the right college with the right system for him. And getting to be the starter right away."

"I'm sure it's not an easy decision."

"No. And the thought of him continuing to play football and risk a serious injury tears me up inside. It is making me a nervous wreck."

At that point, she turned away from me, and I sensed, without needing to be told, that our time for the session today was up.

\*

I stepped out into the blistering heat, and then quickly ducked back inside the air-conditioned lobby. The temperature had shot up past ninety degrees and the air was now dry and still. I had felt my phone vibrate at least three times when I was talking with Dr. Greenland, but decided she would be offended had I bothered to answer. Looking down at my phone now, I saw who had been calling. I punched the button to call back. He answered on the first ring.

"Burnside. It's about time."

"Hello to you, too, Earl."

"My wife said you were here last night. I didn't expect you to drop by."

"I was in the neighborhood. Sorry I didn't call first. I'm like that sometimes. Do you want to meet now? I'm in Pasadena."

Earl hesitated. "I have a tee time in an hour," he said slowly. "Nah, let's just do this by phone."

"All right. Terrible thing that happened at St. Dismas yesterday. I'm sure you've heard."

"Yeah, of course. Tragic. But the world doesn't stop," he said, barely missing a beat. "So you find out who's been skimming my money over there?"

I moved the phone away from my ear and looked at it. The degree of sympathy being exhibited was eye-opening. "No," I said, returning the phone back into position. "Not yet."

"What have you learned? Remember I told you I wanted to know everything about everything."

"I remember. And it's obvious Duke Savich knows something, but he's not about to talk. Same with Curly Underwood. Add in the principal of the school, too, Mularkey. They're all pretty tight-lipped."

"Damn school's a bunch a thieves is what I figure. What else you got?"

"Look, let me ask you something. How well do you know Dash Farsakian's mother?"

"Skye? Oh, hell, everyone knows Skye. Wait a minute. You think she has something to do with this?"

"I don't know. What do you think?"

"Can't imagine. She's too honest. Or maybe too dumb. But Wally's got a restaurant. Pretty successful at one time. Hell, I wouldn't have thought they needed the money. But who knows, you know? Anything's possible, I guess she could have skimmed off the top. She ran the fundraisers, after all. You never know."

I thought about this for a moment. Having money doesn't exclude someone as a suspect when it comes to theft. Some people steal because they have a secret habit, usually gambling or drugs. Some steal because their stream of income has been temporarily cut off. And some do it, well, just because they can. In my freshman year at USC, stereos were being swiped out of rooms in my dormitory. At least half a dozen students were victimized. The campus police surmised it was someone from the surrounding area, a blighted district near downtown L.A. The school limited access to the building and posted a security guard in the lobby to ward off anyone from the neighborhood. But as it turned out, the culprit was a kid from Newport Beach, a fellow student who lived in the dorm. His parents owned a multimillion dollar home, and they sent him checks every month for spending money. He didn't need the cash; he was stealing for the thrill of it, the adrenaline rush that comes with sneaking into someone else's room and grabbing property. He was doing it as a test, simply to see if he could get away with it. But when he was finally apprehended, the kid ended up being kicked out of the University in mid-semester. He then had to find a new college to which he could transfer, one that wouldn't object to a student with a freshly minted criminal record.

"I spoke with Skye briefly the other day," I said. "The more I poke around, the more I get a sense she's involved in something that's not so terrific. I don't know what that is yet."

"Ah, look, she's a good ol' gal," Earl said. "I honestly think you're barking up the wrong tree. I can vouch for that family. They're good people. You look into Noah Greenland and his family? That bunch always bothered me."

"I have looked into them. They're ... a little unusual," I managed. "I haven't met the father yet, but they're not your typical football family."

"They're a bunch of nut jobs," Earl declared. "Something's wrong with them."

"I wouldn't know," I said.

"You keep poking around," Earl ordered. "I want some answers here. I want to get something more for all that money I'm paying you."

And with that, he hung up. I hadn't bothered to tell him about my altercation with Coach Savich, or that Jason Fowler was rumored to have been sexually involved with someone, possibly a student, and it may have cost him his life. How all that was tied to some missing funds was a mystery, but I was keenly aware that murder is frequently tied to either money or sex. Sometimes both.

I headed back to Mar Vista. Marcus was home from his morning at preschool, and our nanny busied herself with cleaning up his room, which was forever strewn with toys. Marcus and I went outside to shoot baskets on his four-foot-high hoop, and I lifted him up a few times to allow for some slam dunks. We read a few stories together before Gail came home, but soon the fatigue of an early day caught up with me. I encouraged Marcus to take a nap, and when he finally went down, I sneaked in a nap, too. But my to-do list still had one more item slated. After a quick dinner, I kissed my family goodnight and headed out to Santa Monica.

The Shutters hotel sat right at the end of Pico Boulevard, facing the beach. The small driveway area for valet parking belied a hotel whose grand and imposing structure could best be appreciated from the sand. Strolling up into the dining room for a minute, I admired the enormous bay windows that let in a flood of light. The sun was still high, and about half the tables were full. A small bar area sat off to one side, and I made a note of it in case my subjects went in here for dinner. I walked back down into the lobby, found myself a soft, comfortable seat facing the front entrance, and waited.

There was a lot of activity, as guests were checking in, going up to the dining room, or simply heading out to the beach. I spent half an hour watching a variety of well-attired and well-coiffed guests amble about. For most of the time it was mind-numbingly boring, although I did have the good fortune to see Willie Nelson, braided ponytail and all, saunter by with a couple of nice-looking women in tow. A few people waved to him as he made his way out, but this being L.A., no one approached. Celebrities usually didn't get bothered much in places like this, as most people choose not to infringe upon their privacy. Doing so would label you an opportunist, or even worse, a tourist.

Rebecca Linzmeier had sent me a photo of her boyfriend, and I took it out of its envelope and studied it. He had a round, handsome face, a full head of sandy blond hair, and a smooth smile. He was middle-aged and looked successful. And as I sat in the well-appointed lobby for half an hour, I saw a number of gentlemen walk in who looked surprisingly similar to, although not quite like, the man I came here to shadow. But finally he arrived.

Doug Trueblood was dressed in a light blue shirt, open at the throat, and wore dressy beige slacks. His hair was neatly combed and he maintained a relaxed expression. In his hand was a white envelope, the type that might hold a Hallmark card. He walked in a relaxed way, but his eyes were focused straight ahead. He wasn't looking around. He seemed to know exactly where he was going, which is to say the bank of elevators at the far end of the lobby. He pressed a button and waited.

In conducting surveillance work, maintaining a hidden identity is critical. When tailing someone, the investigator never wants his presence to be revealed, and certainly doesn't want be alone with the subject, as his cover could be immediately and forever compromised. At some point, the investigator might need to tail the person again, and remaining cloaked anonymously in the background was imperative. The last thing needed was anyone's suspicions being raised.

I turned and watched Doug enter the elevator with three other guests. No contact or acknowledgment was made. The elevator doors closed and that was that. I walked over and noticed the elevator stopped at the third floor and then the fourth floor before heading back to the lobby, empty.

I sighed and found another chair, this one facing the elevator and not nearly as comfortable. I pulled out my phone and scanned the news, my email, and various football sites. The Chicago Bears were opening the season at home on Monday night against the Dallas Cowboys. I set the DVR to record it. I checked my email, checked the weather for the next five days, and texted Gail that I loved her. It took about 30 minutes for her to text me back with a similar sentiment. Oddly, it was a nervous 30 minutes for me. We had been married four years, and I still had to pinch myself that a girl like that would ever end up with someone like me.

After about an hour, Doug Trueblood emerged from the elevator, the same pleasant expression covering his face. His clothes were not rumpled, his hair was not mussed.

That didn't mean he didn't engage in a torrid bout of nocturnal pleasure; it only meant there were no obvious signs of dishevelment. He walked out onto the curb, waited for the valet to fetch his car, and he drove off. I waited five minutes before going to get my Pathfinder. I took a final look around at the splendid lobby and noted the amount of time I had wasted this evening. I called Rebecca Linzmeier and gave her my report. She listened intently. When I was finished, she told me she needed some time to digest all of this and hung up. I looked at my phone for a long three seconds. Then I drove home and went quickly to sleep.

\*

One plus that came with rising early was being able to take advantage of the time zone difference when calling back East. After rolling out of bed, I made a pot of coffee and took a cup into the den. I had thought Johnny Cleary would be busy most of the day with the Bears' preparation for Monday's game. Fortunately for me, he picked up on the first ring.

"Burnside. How've you been?" he yelled into the phone.

"Trying to stay out of trouble."

"Well, getting into trouble was always one of your gifts."

"Ah, you know me too well," I laughed. I was indulging in one of life's hidden treasures, the gift of being able to talk with someone you've known for decades. You can go an extraordinary amount of time without speaking with them, but when you do, the years slip away effortlessly. And with Johnny Cleary, it was as if we were hanging out once again at Heritage Hall.

"Indeed," Johnny said. "How are you adjusting to life after USC?"

"I was going to ask you the same thing."

"I'll tell you. The NFL is a very different ballgame. It's still X's and O's but the guys here are at another level. At SC we had a lot of good players, but in the league, everyone is really good. They know it, and they also know they have a short shelf life to make a pile of dough. So they take it seriously. That's the good part."

"And the bad part?" I asked.

"They're demanding, they're pissy, and they don't shrink when a coach yells at them. In fact, they're a lot more apt to yell back. Receivers want to know why passes aren't being thrown to them, running backs want more touches, quarterbacks complain when someone misses a block. I understand their careers are at stake. But it is hyper-competitive. I'm even looking over my shoulder at the assistant coaches. Got to make sure they've got my back."

"Didn't have to worry about that with me," I laughed.

"Nope, you weren't after my job," Johnny said. "The money's great here, I have to admit. A couple of years doing this, and I'll be set for life."

"If you want to retire that is."

"I know. I don't want to spend the rest of my life playing golf. I also don't have a lot of other skills. Not like you, Mr. Detective."

"Private investigator. But yeah, I can always fall back on this. Which is part of why I'm calling."

"Oh?" he asked.

"I'm investigating something at St. Dismas in Pasadena. You remember Noah."

"Sure. Noah Greenland. We'd been recruiting him for years. One of my spies saw him throw the ball in a flag football game. Couldn't have been more than twelve at the time. He was the real deal even then. But his family situation is messy, if I recall."

"You recall right," I sighed. "His father used to coach at St. Dismas. Got canned for behavioral problems."

"I remember," Johnny said. "The dad is the real piece of work. Has some anger issues. My guess is that's why he married a shrink, to try and work them out."

I laughed and started wondering what the underlying psychological implications were of my marrying an attorney. When we met, Gail was also working in law enforcement, not with the LAPD, but as a campus security officer. I didn't think I was drawn to her because she wore a uniform. I thought I simply fell in love with her eyes and her smile. Maybe there was some other more powerful attraction beneath the surface, but I didn't know what. Perhaps some mysteries might be better left unsolved.

"Do people who do that ever work out their issues?" I asked.

"I don't know. In this case, probably not."

"Johnny, let me ask you something. Rumor has it Duke Savich was actively shopping Noah, trying to leverage him into getting a college coaching gig himself. We both know of a few high school coaches who move up the ladder this way, but you rarely hear them be overly brazen. Any truth to it? Noah committed to SC and then decommitted when you left for the Bears."

Johnny sighed. "Savich tried to pull that on us. But I wasn't about to have a guy like him on our staff. I told him flat out. And he was pissed at Noah for committing to SC. Although not as much as the kid's dad was. I knew this situation was going to be a problem down the road."

"How so?"

"Bob was trying to shop Noah around himself. His own kid. But he wasn't aiming for a coaching job. He wanted a quarter of a million for Noah to sign."

I let out a low whistle. There have been a myriad of instances when alumni of certain schools, working in concert with the coaches, have bribed families to claim the star athlete for their college. In some coaching circles, there was even a saying, that if you're not cheating, you're not trying. But monetizing your child was different. That a parent would take this extraordinary step was unusual, although everything about becoming a father was new to me. I drew on things I learned from teachers, coaches, and anyone who seemed to have an understanding of what being a parent meant. I thought I was doing okay so far. From the picture being painted in front of me, it was clear I could do worse.

Johnny continued. "I didn't tell you or the other assistants about it, no sense poisoning the well for Noah. When he committed to SC, he did it on his own, probably to spite the parents, certainly to spite Savich. I think the kid has some anger issues in him, too. Least as far as I could tell. He just lets it out in a different way. Shrinks call it passive-aggressive. He fights with someone without being direct. But I'll tell you, it was nice to blow a hole in those grand plans that Duke and Bob had for themselves. At least for a while."

"And then you departed," I said.

"Yeah. Everything changed. Noah wasn't so keen on playing for my successor. I always told kids, same as you did, that they should commit to the school, not to the coach. Coaching is not a solid career. Things change for us. For them it should be all about the school. If they're lucky, they'll be with a coach who's good for them and it'll last four or five years. And then the experience they have can extend for a lifetime. Sometimes it happens. I hope it will for Noah. Kid deserves a better shake than what he's gotten so far."

## *Seven*

Kickoff was a few minutes away and Pasadena glowed in the soft orange warmth of a honeyed sunset. The stands were nearly full as I climbed to a seat in the top row of the bleachers, which enabled me to have a good view of the field, but also kept me away from the college scouts. I was growing tired of having to say I was no longer in the business and being unable to offer up a satisfactory reason as to why. An assistant at a successful college football program was only in demand for so long, perhaps a season or two. Sitting up high also meant I got to avoid Mitzi and Earl Bainbridge, who took their seats right at the fifty yard line. They brought along a picnic basket, thermos, and ice chest, and showed little compunction about plopping them down directly onto a pair of seats in a prime location. One parent offered them a dirty look as he inched by, looking for a place to sit, but that was the extent of the chastening. Earl Bainbridge barely took notice.

St. Dismas came out onto the field in their dark green jerseys and matching pants, their gold helmets shiny, if not glowing. De La Salle was decked out in white, with silver helmets and green trim. This was the opening game for both teams, and each were nationally ranked. How someone took thousands of high schools and narrowed them down to the top 25 teams in the nation was beyond me. It was hard enough to do this in college, and there are only a hundred or so schools to choose from. I noticed Duke Savich pacing the sidelines, wearing a baseball cap, a large pair of sunglasses, and a set of headphones that covered most of his face. I also noticed what looked like a bandage above his jaw. I glanced around for any uniformed cops who might be lurking nearby to pick up a certain private investigator on assault charges. Fortunately, things looked safe.

A couple of teenage girls climbed up the bleachers and sat a few feet away from me. They were both pretty and blonde and looked surprisingly alike. The main difference I could discern was one had blue eyes and the other had green. I listened to them for a while as they chatted about school, teachers, and of course, boys. When I heard Austin Bainbridge's name mentioned, I wanted to jump in, but not being prepared with a well-rehearsed opening line that would sound casual, I feared being labeled a pervert, so I stayed quiet. Finally, the marching band appeared, and the drum major directed everyone to stand as they played the national anthem. When the band finished, the momentary lull in the girls' conversation gave me an opening.

"What year are you girls in?" I asked as we sat back down.

"Oh, we're in 11th grade," the blue-eyed one said unenthusiastically and told me her name was Jasmine. The other introduced herself as Ivy. "Looking like the worst year of our lives."

"How so?"

"Nothing but schoolwork. Supposed to be overwhelming."

I told them I felt their pain. Then I changed the subject. "You have boyfriends at the school?" I asked nosily.

Ivy shrugged. "I've gone out with a few."

"Any on the football team?" I asked.

"Are you a parent?"

"Yes, but not here."

"Oh," she said, a little confused. "Are you a college scout or something?"

"Yeah," I said with a vague smile. "Something,"

"I went out with Kirk Rucker a few times," Ivy said. "He's one of the linebackers. Number 53."

"How about Austin Bainbridge? I heard his name mentioned."

The two looked at each other and giggled. Jasmine spoke. "Austin's the shit."

Having spent the past three years immersed in the lexicon of college students, I knew this phrase indicated something good. Being "the shit" was something to aspire to. Being shit was not. Without my three years as a college coach, my uninitiated middle-aged brain would still be struggling to figure out what on earth she was talking about.

"You ever go out with him?" I asked.

"Austin's working his way through our class," Jasmine giggled. "I'm ignoring him for now. It piques guys' interest when you don't pay attention to them. I'll let him get to me eventually. Maybe around prom time."

I smiled. "Smart. What about Dash Farsakian? Is he going out with anyone?"

"He used to go out with our friend Vicki. But they broke up. He's got mommy issues," she said dismissively.

"His parents are getting divorced," Ivy added. "I kind of feel sorry for him."

"I'm not hearing Noah's name. I guess you know every college in the country wants him."

They nodded in unison, looked at each other, and then Ivy finally spoke. "He's just got issues."

A whistle blew and we turned our attention to the field. The teams had lined up for the opening kickoff, with St. Dismas set to receive. They returned the kick to the twenty-two yard line and the special teams trotted off, replaced by the starting units. Both teams looked like they had at least fifty players milling about on the sidelines. A dozen cheerleaders went into an elaborate routine that ended in a cry of "Go Warriors!"

St. Dismas lined up quickly and Noah Greenland surveyed the defense as he stood over center. He took a deep breath and bent down to bark signals. The first two plays were handoffs to the running backs which went nowhere. On third down, Noah took the snap and faded back into the pocket to throw a pass. But the blocking quickly broke down and one of the defensive linemen charged straight at him. Making a nifty move, Noah eluded the defender and scrambled to his right. But no receiver was open downfield, and the lineman regained his head of steam. He crashed into Noah just as he was moving his arm forward. Showing a surprising amount of strength, Noah held the lineman off with a stiff left arm and flung the ball downfield. It traveled about thirty yards down the far sideline, but there was no St. Dismas receiver nearby and the football dropped right in the hands of a De La Salle safety. The defender intercepted the pass, made sure he came down with one foot in bounds, and then began jumping up and down as the De La Salle bench erupted in celebration.

Noah and his teammates walked dejectedly off the field. Noah's head was down and Duke Savich went over and pointed a finger at his quarterback and began to berate him. I wasn't sure Noah was listening. Players who make this type of error sometimes need a little space to clear their head. They knew all too well they had made a mistake. Noah listened, said nothing, and then walked dejectedly over to the bench to sit down by himself. A few players came by to slap his helmet lightly in an encouraging way.

The De La Salle fans were up and cheering, but on the St. Dismas side of the bleachers, it was mostly silent. One middle-aged man a few rows below me stood up and began yelling down at the field. The man was tall and bulky, sporting a shaved head and a deep tan. The top of his skull was red and ruddy and shiny. He had the look of someone who spent a lot of time outdoors. The woman next to him was Stacy Greenland, so it didn't take much to figure out who the boisterous figure was.

"Don't try to force it, Noah!" he yelled. "Take a damn sack if you have to!"

Stacy Greenland tugged on her husband's wrist and implored him to take his seat and keep it down. Instead, he kept up a steady banter. I decided he'd be more interesting to listen to than a pair of teenage girls, so I climbed down a few rows and sat behind them.

"I can't believe what I just saw. First pass of the season, cripes. I told him he needs to keep his picks down this year."

"Bob, please. I'm sure he feels bad enough."

"That idiot coach sent the tailback out on a wheel route. No one was there to pick up the blitz," he sneered as he finally sat down. "What a moron. That Savich has turned into a disaster."

The rest of the first half did not go much better for St. Dismas or for Noah Greenland. He completed some long throws, showing off a powerful arm, but he also misfired on a few. De La Salle was ahead 10-0 as the half neared, with less than a minute to go on the clock. St. Dismas began getting a drive going as Noah completed a number of passes and they moved the ball past midfield. But then De La Salle came with an all-out blitz, sending eight defenders charging in at Noah. He whirled around and threw the ball blindly downfield, where it was intercepted again. The defender cut back across the field and ran through what seemed like the entire St. Dismas team on his way to a touchdown. The De La Salle team was now in full celebratory mode, but missed the yellow flag that lay where Noah had released the ball, a marker that had been thrown down by the referee well after the interception.

"Late hit," announced the referee, as he made a signal banging his forearms together. "Roughing the passer. Defense. Fifteen-yard penalty. No touchdown. The interception is nullified. First down, St. Dismas."

As the referee turned to give the first-down signal, the De La Salle team erupted in angry protest. It was obvious Noah had been hit immediately after he released the ball, which was usually not considered a penalty. De La Salle's coaches argued vehemently, even after the ref had turned away from them, and then may have uttered the wrong word. The referee threw his yellow flag again for unsportsmanlike conduct, another fifteen yard penalty, which now put the ball inside the twenty yard line. The episode reminded me of an incident once when I was playing for USC and got flagged for pass interference. I tried to protest the call, but the referee just smiled at me and asked if I knew when a penalty was correct. It stopped me for a second and I said no. He laughed and responded that it's a penalty when he says it's a penalty. This was a lesson that stayed with me forever, and it was the last time I argued with an official. After that, I simply tried to act friendly with them.

It took a few minutes for the referees to restore some semblance of order and for the teams to get set again. Noah lined up in the shotgun formation, standing a few yards behind the center. He took the snap and looked downfield. Finding a receiver open near the corner of the end zone, he fired a laser strike, and the ball hit Austin Bainbridge in the chest. Austin wore number 19 and the ball literally landed smack between the one and the nine. But rather than gathering it in, the ball bounced off of Austin's chest and floated up in the air. It felt like an eternity but it reality took only about a second for the football to land in the arms of a De La Salle player, for another interception, although this one did not get returned for a touchdown. An audible groan was emitted by the partisan crowd, and the St. Dismas players trudged to the sidelines as the first half ended. The teams then went off into their respective locker rooms.

"I swear, I can't believe this," Bob Greenland fumed. "This is supposed to be Noah's moment. The game's being televised. I ought to go down into that locker room and talk to this team. They look like a sinking ship right now."

"Bob, you can't do that," Stacy implored. "You know the agreement."

"I just don't want Noah to blow this opportunity. Everything's going wrong. Savich is dialing up the wrong plays and the team isn't responding. This is bad. This is awful. Noah's drowning out there."

"Look," she said, "it's not like any college is going to pull their offer. Stanford said their scholarship was solid."

"Stanford," he hissed. "That's all I hear from you. Stanford. Yeah, sure, it's a good school, but who cares? It's not the best fit for Noah right now. And they're not offering anything beyond a scholarship. And schools can pull their offer anytime they want before Signing Day in February."

"I just think you need to be careful. Remember what happened last time you pushed Noah too hard."

"I know, I know. He went off and committed to USC. That's the last thing I want."

I took in a deep breath and cleared my throat in such an affected way that people a section over might have heard me. The Greenlands turned around to see who was making the ruckus.

"Oh," said Stacy, involuntarily wrinkling her nose. "It's you."

"Yes, it's me. Hello to you, too."

Her husband peered at me. "You're that USC guy."

"You have a good memory. Sorry our offer to Noah didn't meet your requirements."

"Uh, look," Bob said, his voice dropping. "We don't need to rehash all that. Let's leave it in the past."

"I suppose. Of course, someone once said the past is never dead, it's not even the past."

"You sound like my wife," he muttered. "That's what a psychologist would say."

I smiled. "Actually it was William Faulkner. Maybe he studied some psychology in college."

"Mr. ... Burnside, was it?" Stacy Greenland asked, sounding a little miffed. "Is there anything we can help you with?"

"Nope. I'm just a guy sitting here."

The teams returned to the field, and St. Dismas kicked off. The second half was looking a lot like the first until the middle of the 4th quarter, when seemingly out of nowhere, Noah reared back and threw a long pass to

Austin, who ran under it for a touchdown. With the deficit cut to 10-7, the St. Dismas defense stiffened, and De La Salle punted the ball back to them with four minutes to go in the game. Noah stepped back onto the field and looked ready to lead his team down the field on a game-winning drive. He completed a few short passes to position the team near midfield, one yard away from a first down. Noah faked a handoff and dropped back to pass. And then it happened. The defense wasn't fooled by the fake, or at least one player wasn't. A very large, very athletic defensive lineman spun past his blocker and barreled toward Noah as he drew his arm back to throw the ball. Lowering his head, the lineman launched himself into Noah, smashing him square on the chin with the crown of his helmet. You could hear the ugly thud from the bleachers. It was an illegal hit, but the damage was done. Noah managed to hold onto the ball, but landed smack on his back and didn't get up.

A wave of stunned silence came over the crowd. Noah lay motionless on the turf, and the coaches and trainers raced onto the field. They worked on him for a few minutes before he was able to get to his feet on his own, and walk shakily toward the sideline. The crowd sighed and gave him a round of applause, but that would be it for Noah tonight. A backup quarterback pulled on a helmet and took his place. De La Salle was penalized fifteen yards for roughing the passer again, but the new quarterback was unable to even complete a single pass, and St. Dismas turned the ball over on downs. De La Salle ran out the clock, and the game ended with St. Dismas on the losing end of a 10-7 score, and Noah Greenland walked unsteadily across the field toward the dark gloom of a losing locker room.

\*

Since it wasn't my team that was defeated, I didn't suffer any special loss of sleep that night, other than from the usual parade of private jets warming up early. Marcus appeared to be taking after his father as an early riser, waking up right after dawn. We played two games of hide-and-go-seek, which Marcus won handily, and then we watched an animal show together on TV. This particular episode featured a pot-bellied pig that someone had chosen to take in as a pet. It showed the happy owner proudly walking his pig on a leash in his neighborhood, garnering the attention and admiration of everyone he came into contact with.

I thought back to when I worked vice in North Hollywood, and to a certain civilian employee of the LAPD. His daughter thought it would be cute to have a monkey for a pet, so he got her one. That experiment lasted three days, a debacle which included the monkey bringing down a chandelier which he thought was there for him to swing on. Monkeys are considered among the smartest of animals, but their actions are not easy to figure out. This one thought it was great fun to grab a bowl of mac and cheese and throw it all over the kitchen. The culmination of the experiment was when the family discovered the monkey had no qualms about treating the living room as his own personal toilet. So when Marcus began his campaign to get a pot-bellied pig as a pet, I was prepared with an answer. And at just that moment, Chewy, our black cocker spaniel, came into the living room and greeted us with a big yawn. She went over and laid down with her head on Marcus's lap, and that seemed to be enough to quell, for the moment, any further need for an additional pet.

This being a Saturday afternoon in September, there was a UCLA football game scheduled at the Rose Bowl. I waited until a few minutes before kickoff before climbing into my Pathfinder and making what would have surely been an arduous journey up to Pasadena had I left a few hours earlier. The worst time to arrive in Pasadena was two or three hours before the start of a football game. The fans were all over town, eating in restaurants, drinking in pubs, and clogging up street traffic to a frustrating level. Pasadena never feels smaller than when 90,000 football fans descend upon it and overrun the city. But once the visitors have made the long trek down into the Arroyo Seco basin and become ensconced in their seats, the city resumed its quiet ways.

Up until the early 1980s, USC and UCLA football teams shared the L.A. Coliseum, but it was always more of a USC venue. Nestled practically in SC's backyard, the Coliseum was a natural home for the Trojans, but an inconvenient drive for UCLA students. Following a testy disagreement with the Coliseum Commission, UCLA moved its football games to the Rose Bowl venue, which was even *more* inconvenient than the Coliseum, but at least it gave the

Bruins their own home, one they didn't have to share with their cross-town rivals. At USC, we were happy enough they were gone, even if they had decamped to the fabled Rose Bowl. We only wanted to play in Pasadena once a year. On New Year's Day.

I pulled up in front of Skye Farsakian's house, a few blocks from the Bainbridge Estate. It was a nice modern home, although it didn't start out that way. Part of the house maintained the austere look of an old Pasadena Craftsman, with multiple gables sticking out here and there, but another section of the home had been updated recently. This happened all too frequently with remodeled homes in California. Many years ago, Proposition 13 froze the property value from which taxes were assessed, but if the house was torn down and a new one erected, the property value shot up to market rates. Wealthy homeowners who wanted to build a big new home on their land, but didn't want to pay big tax rates could do so by tearing down most of the structure -- except for one wall. The law stated that if at least one wall were left standing, it was not considered a new home, and the property value could not be re-assessed. Meaning taxes on the home would remain at the same low level as they had been for decades. So many of these homeowners simply left one wall of the house intact, tore down the rest, and put up a freakish-looking McMansion, one that maintained low property taxes, but effectively gave them a brand new home. Californians really aren't crazy. We just play according to an unusually designed rulebook.

The refurbished Ford Mustang that Dash Farsakian was driving the other night was parked in the driveway, next to a not-quite-as-old Porsche Targa. In front of the house sat a dark blue BMW. It was hard to tell how old it was. That was the beauty of a BMW, the style didn't change that much over the years. Unless someone kept current with the subtle changes in the newer models, this was a car that could easily impress others.

I knocked on the door, and a barrel-chested man wearing only a black t-shirt and a light blue bathing suit answered the door. In his hand was a can of Budweiser.

"Can I help you?" he asked.

"Yes, I'm here to see Skye. The name's Burnside."

"What do you want?"

"I think I'd want to talk with Skye. Who are you?"

"I'm her husband. Now just who the hell are you?"

"Like I said. The name's Burnside," I told him and flashed my fake gold shield.

"Oh," he said, the insolence leaving his voice.

"I spoke with your wife the other day. I'm conducting an investigation regarding St. Dismas."

"What kind of an investigation?"

"It's about some fundraising irregularities," I said, leaving out the part that might include an association, however marginal, to the murder of a teacher. "We're not investigating your wife. But she worked on some fundraisers and I'd like to ask her some questions."

"I don't know about this," he started.

"We could do it here or down at the police station," I said evenly, not bothering to tell Mr. Farsakian that I had nothing to do with the Pasadena police. Or that if Hugh Turco knew, he would probably have me arrested for impersonating a police officer, not to mention interfering with an ongoing murder case.

"All right," he sighed and opened the door. "Skye's at the pool. My son has a few friends over."

"Thanks. Your name?"

"I'm Wally. Wally Farsakian."

We walked through the house and onto the patio leading to a large pool with a Jacuzzi nearby. It was a hot day and I would have loved to have jumped in. The pool was blue and inviting, and there were a half dozen very large teenagers happily engaged, either splashing each other in the water or doing cannonballs off of the diving board.

"So I was under the impression you were getting divorced," I said pleasantly, as we walked toward the pool.

"We're separated. Trying to work stuff out. But we're on civil terms. And I like spending time with Dash. Even if it's just watching him horseplay with his friends. Teenagers and all. They don't like hanging around with their parents at this age. Harder to see him when you're not even living at home. I'm supposed to get him every other weekend, but you know, with football, he's a busy kid."

"I understand," I said, mentally praying I would never, ever be in that situation.

"And I work nights in my restaurant. Valley Steakhouse. You should come by some time," he said with a restrained degree of enthusiasm. "It's a great place."

Skye Farsakian was seated at a white plastic patio table that was shaded by a green and gold umbrella. She sipped a tall red drink through a straw. Skye wore large sunglasses and had on a sheer pool dress that had the thickness of a dragonfly's wing. It was designed to not hide anything, and it clearly succeeded. The skimpy white bikini she wore was in full, glorious view. I had to look twice to make sure it was a swimsuit and not lingerie. I also had to remind myself that staring was impolite.

"Hello there," I managed.

"Oh, hi. I remember you."

"Skylar, this man says he's conducting an investigation."

"I actually am conducting an Investigation," I told him. "Just for the record."

"Yes," she said. "We met this week at practice. You were looking into something regarding fundraising. Did you find out anything?"

"Not yet. But I'm also looking into what happened the other day. Jason Fowler."

"Oh, my."

"I was one of the last people to have seen him," I said. "I went to talk with Mary Swain that evening, like you suggested, but she was gone. So I spoke with Mr. Fowler for a while."

"I see," she said and turned to her husband, or perhaps, soon-to-be ex-husband. "Wally, would you mind bringing our guest something cold to drink?"

Wally looked suspiciously at her. "Why?"

"Because he's a guest and it's rude not to," she said. "What would you like? Beer? A Coke?"

"A Coke would be fine," I said, and Wally walked off unenthusiastically.

Once Wally was out of earshot, Skye Farsakian removed the sunglasses and looked at me. Her bright blue eyes were big and strikingly beautiful, and the last time I saw eyes this pretty, they belonged to Judy Atkin. I was taken aback for a second, but Skye quickly got me to refocus.

"So how do I fit into all this?" she asked coolly, her voice not nearly as coquettish as the other day.

"I'm not sure you do," I said, trying to reassure her, or at least get her to drop her guard for a moment. "But from what I can gather, Mr. Fowler was very friendly around the girls."

"Oh?" she said, feigning surprise in a way that bad actors are prone to do. "Do you mean he was involved with one of them?"

"I'm thinking so, yes. And I'm thinking that had something to do with his being murdered."

Skye put a hand over her mouth. "Good heavens. Who do you think it was?"

"I'm not sure. Does the name Vicki ring a bell?"

"Yes, Vicki Sailor, of course. Dash went out with her for a while. But she was such a sweetheart. Could she have had anything to do with this? I guess people always surprise you."

"Maybe, maybe not. Any other girls who might have had an involvement with Mr. Fowler? Even a harmless flirtation? Something that could have been misconstrued?"

"No, I wouldn't have any idea."

"All right. Would you happen to have Vicki's contact information? Maybe she didn't have anything to do with this, but I'd like to talk with her."

"Well ... I suppose it would be all right. Don't tell her parents I gave it to you. People can be a little protective of their kids. Maybe a little too much so," she said, scanning through her phone and writing something down on a piece of paper.

"It's nice to have all that information at your fingertips," I mused.

"As a fundraiser, I have a big Rolodex," she said, as she handed the paper to me. "Oh, silly me. We don't use Rolodexes any more. Funny how you can get into a habit, isn't it?"

I smiled and pocketed the paper. Wally Farsakian returned and placed an icy can of 7 Up in front of me. I wondered if they were out of Coke, or, like the police, he wanted to show me who was in charge around here. Or maybe he just didn't know how to listen.

"So," Wally said, "you figure out who bumped off Jason Fowler?"

"Wally!" Skye exclaimed. "That's a horrible way to put it!"

I looked at him and shook my head. "You have any ideas?"

Looking out over the pool, Wally Farsakian thought about the question. Then he took a swig of beer. The teenagers were busy tossing a football, throwing it so the others would have to jump high out of the water to snare it. Most of the time they didn't, and they gave off a loud groan, followed by some raucous laughter.

"I wonder," he said, "if it wasn't one of the football coaches."

"Wally, that's outrageous. You're drunk. Mr. Burnside, don't listen to him."

"Why do you say that?" I asked, ignoring his wife.

"I think maybe Fowler had something on one of the coaches. Doing something he shouldn't."

"Like what?"

Wally looked back at me. "You said you were looking into fundraising issues. There's some funny things going on there. Skye raised a ton of money and it's not being spent. I'll bet Jason knew. I'll bet he had something on them."

I sighed to myself. Back to square one. I heard a phone begin to ring, and remarkably, one of the teenagers in the pool heard it, too. Pulling himself out, he sloshed water onto the cement and raced over to pull the phone out of a green backpack. He was an exceptionally large kid, another lineman undoubtedly, and his belly jiggled as he moved. He spoke into the phone and then his mouth opened and his facial expression froze for a few seconds. He spoke quietly into the phone and then put it down.

"Hey, guys," he yelled. "Hey. Knock it off. Quiet down. You got to hear this."

"What? You gonna eat another two pizzas by yourself today?" one of them yelled.

"No, you idiot. Shut up. That was Will, he's at the hospital."

"What happened?" Dash asked, and the group grew quiet.

"It's Noah."

"What about Noah? They rule it a concussion?"

"Not that. He was rushed to the E.R. last night. Noah swallowed a bottle of sleeping pills."

# *Eight*

There is something very impressive about the architecture of modern hospitals, and Huntington Memorial was no exception. Whether it was the arched steel-and-glass frame lining the exterior entranceway or the soaring magnificence of the glass-lined atrium which served as a lobby, an extraordinary amount of care and money had been invested in offering hospital visitors the feeling they were entering into a shining beacon of hope. No expense had been spared when it came to presenting the grandiose shrine to modern medical care. If someone needed to visit a patient at Huntington Memorial today, they were left with the comforting feeling that the person would be looked after quite well.

I went up to the fourth floor, and it didn't take long to see the crowd congregating around Room 416. A group of a dozen middle-aged folks, along with a similar number of teenagers, loitered nervously about the hallway. As I approached, a nurse in dark blue scrubs came by and informed everyone they needed to head to the waiting room. They were blocking the medical personnel from moving freely down the hallway, and what's more, Noah Greenland wasn't taking visitors right now.

As we entered the waiting room, small groups began to form. I approached a nice-looking couple, who had not yet engaged anyone in conversation. The man was tall and broad-shouldered, and wore a golf shirt and khakis; the woman was pretty and wore a sundress. They looked like any other successful, suburban, middle aged parents. I smiled sadly at them and said hello. They proffered an odd look in return.

"Have you heard anything about Noah's condition?" I asked.

"Yes," the man replied after a moment's pause. "He's stable. Looks like he's going to pull through. I guess they got him here quickly and pumped his stomach. He'll be okay."

"Good to hear," I said.

"Do we know you?"

"I'm sorry, no," I said and flashed my fake gold shield. The couple's posture stiffened, and their facial expressions became more serious. They introduced themselves as Buzz and Talley Kingston.

"My name is Burnside. I'm doing an investigation here. Maybe you could help."

"I'm not so sure," Talley Kingston said tentatively. "We only know what everyone else here knows."

"Which is?" I asked officiously.

"Well," Talley began, "we heard Stacy went to check on Noah after he said he was going to bed last night. I guess she tends to baby him. She saw an empty bottle of

Dalmane, and put two and two together. They couldn't wake Noah up, so they called an ambulance and rushed him here. Like Buzz just said, he's going to pull through. Frankly, I think the parents are in worse shape. Bob and Stacy are beside themselves now. All that worry. I know I'd be frightened out of my mind if it had been Will."

"Does Will play football?"

"Yes, of course. Everyone here is a parent of a player. It's sort of a cult. Or a clique, I guess."

"So you know the Greenlands well."

"Somewhat. Why?"

"Just wondering," I said. "You never know. Let me ask you something. This had to have been quite a shock, right?"

They looked at each other. "Well, I suppose," Buzz said haltingly. "It never struck anyone that Noah was happy. Except when he was out on the football field. Our son, Will plays linebacker. He told us Noah's a different kid when he's playing. More confident, more sure of himself. It's like his troubles get to stay on the sidelines, and he can put them out of his mind for a while."

"Troubles?"

"Oh," he said. "I don't want to go too into this. It's been a terrible week."

"This is part of a criminal investigation," I reminded him, not bothering to add that the police at one point were considering me as a person of interest in the murder case. "It's related to what happened at the school last week. It's serious. I need to know everything."

"Yes, yes, I suppose. Well, his parents, you know, Bob and Stacy, they're not exactly the most loving couple. You know what they say. Best thing a dad can do for his kids is to love their mother. Gives them a sense of being grounded. Noah never had that. Will used to go over to their house a lot when Noah first came to the school a couple of years ago, they had been friendly. But he said Noah's parents were arguing all the time, and their bickering was just too much. It affected the kids' friendship. Will stopped going there."

"I think it affected a lot of friendships for Noah," Talley jumped in. "Bob's a piece of work."

"How so?"

They glanced at each other again. Talley spoke. "Oh. He made a pass at me once. I declined and gave him a lecture on being appropriate. For his son's sake. He just laughed and said he'd move on to the next one. Just like that. Can you imagine?"

Buzz Kingston looked down and shuffled his feet. "I'd heard they were having money problems. Bob's career's been on the skids. Being a private coach doesn't give much of a steady income stream. Maybe he has too much time on his hands. Anyway, I let it go. If he made a second pass at her, I'd have knocked his block off."

I took this in. "Bob's a big guy."

"I'm a big guy, too. Yeah, I know all about Bob Greenland's reputation when he was a coach. Beat up some parent a few years ago. But I served in the Air Force, I'm not scared of anything. Or anyone."

"Who was the parent?"

"Name was Stan Weekes. Took his kids out of the school, obviously, but he filed a lawsuit. Forced Bob out of coaching."

"I imagine that didn't sit well," I said.

"Serves him right. Bob's a hothead. Doesn't think before he acts. Obviously."

"So tell me. What was Bob's relationship like with his son?"

"Oh, man. Bob was busy planning out Noah's career for him. And his mother was always trying to psychoanalyze him."

I absorbed this for a moment longer than I wanted to. "Is Noah close to anyone at school now?"

"I don't think so. He used to be friends with Dash Farsakian and that crew. But they moved away from him. Probably for the same reason. I think he's close to a few teachers. Ms. Swain was his favorite."

"I've been trying to reach Mary Swain. I've heard she's on leave."

"No one seems to know," she said. "The school's funny like that. Sometimes a coach or a teacher will just stop being there. No reason given. They're just gone. It's almost like they've ceased to exist."

I took a breath and avoided making a crass comment about Jason Fowler. But I needed to raise the subject, and I needed their help. I needed anyone's help. The answer to this puzzle seemed right in front of me, and yet hiding in plain sight.

"I need to bring up a difficult subject. Jason Fowler. I know it's a tough thing to talk about."

"Of course," Buzz said.

"Do you know of anything that was going on with Mr. Fowler and one of his students?"

They both shook their heads. "No. Why?" Talley asked.

"There's been a suggestion he may have had an inappropriate relationship with someone."

"Oh?"

"Has your son mentioned anything about this?"

"No, not necessarily."

"I'm not sure I understand," I said, leaning forward. "Not necessarily?"

"Well, I don't know for certain. But I do know our son mentioned Dash was ticked at Mr. Fowler about something. Might have been a girl. Dash used to go out with this cute little thing. What was her name, Buzz?"

I leaned in further. "Was it Vicki?"

"Yeah. Vicki. Vicki Sailor. I honestly don't know what was going on there. But something was."

\*

I drove to the condo where Vicki Sailor lived, but no one answered when I buzzed the intercom outside the security gate. I went back to the Starbucks on Lake Avenue, and sipped on an iced mocha frappuccino for a while as I worked my iPad, trying to settle on what to do next. Since I was already in Pasadena, I figured I should talk to someone. Anyone.

I found Mary Swain's home easily enough, property titles for homeowners are a matter of public record in

California, and addresses are a breeze to find. So is the price they paid for their house, the purchase date, and the size of their mortgage. This sort of data had always been public; the Internet simply made it astoundingly easy for any nosy person to access.

Mary Swain lived in a small yellow bungalow with chocolate brown trim, the type of color combination that was all the rage about eighty-five years ago. That might well have been the last time it had received a fresh coat of paint as well. The house was situated a few blocks north of Colorado Boulevard., the street which served as the main artery for the Rose Parade each year. I had actually been on Mary Swain's block once, but that was many years ago. A fellow LAPD officer hosted a New Year's Eve party, one which turned into a sleepover for those who wanted to stay on and go watch the parade in person the next morning. Of course, by the time most of us were ready for sleep, the sun was practically coming up. We turned on the TV, calculated when the parade was a block away, and walked down in time to see the colorful floats and the marching bands. I meant to come back and view the parade again, one of a myriad of things I keep planning to do and never quite get around to doing. But now that Marcus was getting old enough to appreciate it, I thought we might take him this year. It would also serve as a nice birthday present. He was born on January 1st.

I rapped on the front door, and it opened quickly. A spry, slender woman in her 50s looked up at me. She was wearing a gray t-shirt, faded jeans, and tennis shoes. Her hair was silver and short.

"Ms. Swain?"

"Yes?"

"The name's Burnside," I said and handed her my card. "May I come in?"

She looked at my card and then back at me. "What can I do for you?"

I licked my lips. "I've been asked to do an investigation into improprieties regarding the St. Dismas football team. There've been some financial issues. I thought you might be able to provide some perspective."

"Well," she said, opening the door and ushering me in. "By all means. And call me Mary."

I entered her living room, which was small, but neat. A throw rug, a couple of chairs, and a small couch filled up much of the room. What was most noticeable was the bookshelf, which took up an entire wall, stretching across the whole room, filled with books from floor to ceiling. I walked over and started browsing. Lots of biographies, books on American history, some historical novels, a mixture of hardcover and paperback. When you examine someone's bookshelf, you learn an awful lot about the person. I recalled being back in Principal Mularkey's office a few days ago. It was quickly obvious the principal's books were a prop, placed there just for show, never having been cracked open. Perhaps they had been shelved for future reading, but often they were there to simply impress. All of the books on Mary Swain's bookshelf, however, had the unmistakable seal of wear, spines broken, books which had not only been opened, but most likely read cover-to-cover.

"Looks like I'm indeed in the home of a history teacher," I said, walking back to a chair and sitting down. Mary Swain sat down across from me.

"Oh, yes. I love history. Loved teaching it and loved learning about it. In the summer, I'd plan my vacations around what books I'd been reading that year. In July, I went to Virginia. I had been reading a lot about the Civil War, so Bull Run and Appomattox were on my list, I wanted to see the battlefield and the courthouse. And while I was there, I went back to Monticello and Mount Vernon. I've been to those before, but you can never see them enough. Not in my opinion, anyway."

"Sounds like a nice vacation," I said.

"It was wonderful. I've been trying to get the school to organize some class trips back East. We used to do those every year, but there've been budget issues lately."

I frowned. "Money problems at a private school?"

"No, not money problems *per se*. Just how the school is deciding to spend their money. That damn football team gets far too much in my opinion. Now what's this about financial improprieties?"

"Uh, yes. I've been hired to look into some missing funds. There was a large fundraiser this spring, and apparently the proceeds have disappeared."

"Someone pull a stick-up?" she smiled.

I smiled back. "No. But I've been asked to look into it. And when I started poking around, your name came up. Not in the sense that you had anything to do with it, of course. Only that you weren't a big fan of the football team."

"I'm not. I think football is dangerous to kids' health and a big distraction from their studies."

"You and my wife might get along," I said, suddenly wishing I hadn't. Football was becoming one of a number of thorny issues I noticed cropping up between Gail and me. We had spent some blissful years together, and I loved her deeply. Then we had Marcus, and as they say, kids change everything. I still loved her, but cracks were emerging in our smooth and shiny relationship. But this wasn't a topic I needed to bring up with a complete stranger and I kicked myself for doing so. A couple's problems should stay between the two of them. And maybe their therapist.

"You're a football fan, Mr. Burnside?"

"I'm afraid it's more involved than that," I said wryly. "I used to play football at SC. And I coached there for three years. I'm pretty tied to the game."

"And you still seem to have emerged with a sound mind. Congratulations."

"Look, Mary," I said. "I'm sure we'll disagree on some things. But I've been hired to try and find out what happened to the funds. And now I'm involved in that tragedy at the school this week. Whether the money's been spent on football or is lining someone's pockets, I'm wondering if there's anything you can share with me. Any path you can send me down. No nugget is too small right now."

Mary Swain sat back and rubbed her hands. "I'm not sure what to tell you. I've had a few dust-ups with those knucklehead coaches. Savich and his big goon,

Underwood. I can't believe they'd be skimming money, though. They're idiots, not thieves. But they've always been asking for special treatment, letting kids take makeup tests because they missed class to go to a game, getting them excused for not handing in homework. Last May they crossed the line. They wanted me to give a passing grade to one of their players who flunked every exam he took. I refused. They said they needed to keep him eligible for football, that it was for the good of the school. I told Savich to go jump in a lake."

"How did he respond?"

"He doesn't care a whit about those kids. Just wants to use them. To advance his own career. I even heard Savich is using one of the players to try and get himself a job coaching at a university. The idea that muttonhead could be working on a college campus turns my stomach."

Having known a lot of college football coaches, I can clearly state that few are ever confused with professors. While coaches can be as articulate and passionate as any academic, they often leave little doubt as to their goals. They are not on campus in the pursuit of knowledge, but rather, in the pursuit of victories.

"Do you mind if I ask who the player was?" I asked, knowing the answer.

"I shouldn't say, but at this point, I don't think I owe that school anything."

"I have a funny feeling this relates to Noah Greenland."

"Yes. Of course it does. Damn shame, too. Kid is so bright, but he's disturbed as hell. Meticulous and sloppy at the same time. He doesn't need football. Football needs him. I thought I was able to get through to him last year. That he needs to make his own choices, not let others do so. That he should forget about football. Leave school with his skull intact."

"It isn't as bad as you're making it out to be," I pointed out.

"Oh, no?"

"Football builds teamwork and discipline. It shows you how you can achieve goals, even if they seem insurmountable. And one other thing. It's also fun."

"I don't think it was fun anymore for Noah," she said. "Maybe when he was younger, before the stakes got so big. Then his parents couldn't agree on whether he should even play football. That's part of his problem. Two parents and they can't agree on a thing. They say opposites attract, but those two are a good argument for how that kind of a marriage can turn into a colossal failure."

"How do you come to know all this?" I asked.

"I take an interest in my kids and I like to help them. Noah was one of my best students last year. You know, history classes are becoming like art and music, disappearing from school curricula, or at least de-emphasized. Some idiots think you just have to drill kids in math and science to be competitive. They forget we're dealing with human beings. And human beings need to be well-rounded."

"True. So you heard what happened to Noah?"

"Yes, I heard. Of course I heard, and I can't say as I'm too surprised. Awful. Simply awful that he had to make that cry for help. Maybe this will be the impetus to get him to quit football. But it's tough. He's getting a lot of pressure. From the coaches, the school, other kids. I think now that his mother has seen the number of scholarships being floated for playing football, she's changed her tune. With college tuition right around the corner, the idea of someone else paying over $65,000 a year to educate your kid has a lot of appeal."

"That's a little cynical," I commented.

"I suppose it might seem that way. I don't have children, so I don't have that financial responsibility. But I'm not blind either. I see it for what it is."

"And speaking of finances, any thoughts as to where this fundraising money might have disappeared?"

Mary Swain thought about this for a minute. "All money raised, no matter for what department, has to go through the school's accounting office. But everything they do needs to be approved by the principal. Mularkey."

"Oh," I said absently, trying to figure out where to go next with this. Then I had an idea. "You seem to know quite a bit. Might someone in Mularkey's office be open with you? Could I ask you to inquire about this?"

"You could, but I'm afraid you're a few days late."

"How so?" I asked, not liking what I sensed was coming.

"After I refused to switch the grades for one of his players at the end of last semester, Savich told me he'd get even."

"Really."

"That's right. And it looks like he did. Last week I got terminated."

I frowned and thought back to my conversation earlier with Jason Fowler. "I heard that you were taking a sabbatical."

"That's just what the school says when they fire someone. The sabbatical never ends, the teacher never returns. Thirty-five years at St. Dismas. Oh, Mularkey gave me a nice severance package and said he'd start my pension right away. That's only to keep me from suing them. But make no mistake. I was fired last week. For trying to do right by the kids."

"I'm sorry to hear that," I said.

"Yes, well, I even recommended Jason take over the department. But you know what happened to him. First Jason, now Noah. They say bad things come in threes, so I can only imagine what will happen next. That school is just swimming in tragedy."

"I'm well aware. Do you have any idea who might have had a reason to do this to Jason?"

Mary Swain sniffed. "Probably one of his floozies."

"Floozies?" I asked, eyebrows raised.

"Oh, right. I believe the word people use today is skanks."

"I know what a floozie is. And a skank. I was just surprised he was involved with more than one."

"Listen, everyone has a weakness. For Jason Fowler it was women. He liked them, they liked him. Didn't matter who they were or how old they were. He had no boundaries in that department."

"I've heard rumors he was involved with a student. A young girl."

166

"I hadn't heard that," Mary said, looking at me curiously. "Although I wouldn't be surprised if he fouled the nest."

"What did you hear?" I asked.

"I heard he was involved with someone at the school. And he was careless about it. But that's about all I know."

\*

I had much better luck the second time I tried the intercom outside of Vicki Sailor's condo. Just off of Sierra Madre, it was a decent building, freshly painted white with blue trim. It was on the small side, containing about a dozen units. The exterior was made of stucco, and it looked like it had been built sometime in the past few decades. Vicki picked up and asked a number of questions, the intercom screeching her voice in a much louder than normal way. After a few back-and-forths, the buzzer sounded and I walked up a flight of stairs to her unit.

I knocked and a slender girl with long, honey blonde hair greeted me. Vicki was pretty, with big brown eyes and a turned-up nose. She wore a sleeveless gray top and volleyball shorts. She looked like an innocent teenager, but looks are all too often deceiving. I needed to learn whether or not she was sexually involved with a teacher or even played some role in his murder. How I'd get her or anyone else to reveal that type of a secret was beyond me right now.

"Hi. Are you Vicki?" I asked.

"I am. Sorry for the suspicion. There's a lot of crazy stuff going on right now. My parents told me to be very careful."

"Understood," I said and handed her my card. Best to leave her with something more tangible than the memory of a fake badge being flashed all-too-quickly. "My name's Burnside. I'm conducting an investigation regarding St. Dismas. Can I ask you a few questions?"

"All right," she said and leaned against the doorway. She made no motion to invite me inside, and even if she had, I had no intention of going there. I didn't even want to ask if her parents were home, lest I raise any concern or fear that I might be after something beyond information. Vicki looked underage, as well as attractive, innocent, and waif-like.

"It won't take long," I assured her.

"It's fine."

"Obviously you know what happened this week with Mr. Fowler," I started.

"Obviously."

"Did you hear about Noah?"

She nodded. "One of my friends called a little while ago. The word's spreading. Do you know how he's doing?"

"I was at the hospital earlier. They say he'll pull through."

"Good. I like Noah. I was a cheerleader last year, so I got to know a lot of the guys on the team. Actually, St. Dismas isn't a big school, so I know pretty much everyone."

"Are you still a cheerleader?"

"Good Lord, no. Getting tossed twenty feet off the ground and having to do twirls in mid-air isn't my idea of a good time. Cheerleading is practically a sport itself these days. For a lot of cheerleaders, the football game is merely a backdrop."

"Uh-huh. So how friendly are you with Noah?" I asked.

"Casual. Enough to know he was unhappy. I mean, I wouldn't have predicted this, but I'm not totally surprised, either. Everyone puts so much pressure on those boys. When the team wins, they're kings, when they lose, they're bums. I don't like that. This is my last year, I'm a senior. I'll be happy to be out of high school soon. Especially after what happened this week."

"It had to have been traumatic. Were you in Mr. Fowler's class?"

"I was. He was a great teacher. And a good guy. I can't believe anyone would do this to him," she said, and I saw her blink away a couple of tears. "I was just telling this to Dash this morning on the phone. We keep talking about it. Everyone's in a state of shock. The school brought in grief counselors, but I don't know how much good they do. It's like I was telling Dash. When someone's gone, they're gone. All you have are memories."

"Dash Farsakian," I said and then asked a question for which I already knew the answer. "Were you close to him?"

"I used to go out with Dash," she said, composing herself a bit.

"Not anymore?"

"No. I've gone out with him off-and-on for a while. Now it's off, probably for good. He's nice, I guess. We're still friendly. No real spark between us, though. But his mother, oh wow. Even if I really liked Dash, being with him meant being with his mom. Even when she wasn't there."

"How do you mean?"

"Well, some guys just want to be taken care of all the time. I guess he's used to that from his mom. She gives him everything, does everything. I swear, that boy doesn't even clear his own dishes when he finishes dinner. I'm into having a boyfriend. But with Dash I'd be more like his second mom than anything else. Not my idea of a relationship."

"You know his mom well?

"Well enough. She waits on him hand-and-foot. And his mom is a little too affectionate."

"With Dash?" I asked cautiously.

She shook her head. "With him, with everyone. I swear, Dash's mom flirts with every man who comes within a mile of her. She'd flirt with a dog if it were a male. That whole scene, it's weird."

"In what way?"

"Oh. When Dash's parents separated last year, it was as if something happened, I don't know, maybe the chains came off her. She started going out with a lot of men," she said and then added, "maybe to prove to herself she's still attractive. I don't know why adults think they have to do this."

I took this in. This was an impressive observation for a teenager. "You seem to have a pretty good understanding of human nature."

"I like psychology," she said and displayed a shy smile. "Everyone's got a calling. Mine seems to be in analyzing people. Trying to help them, although I think psychology is better at helping people figure out why they are the way they are, rather than giving them a plan for going forward."

"Maybe so. Look, when I went over to Dash's house today, I saw his father there. Hanging out. Are his parents back together now?"

"I don't think so," she said. "At least not full time. Sucks for Dash. I think he needs some help. He's got some anger issues. I'm just not trained to help him yet."

"You seem to know a lot about that family."

"More than I want to," she sighed.

"Oh? What else?"

She hesitated and looked down at the ground. "It, um, involves Mr. Fowler."

"What do you mean?"

"He was ... nice to me," she started. "Not in a perv sort of way. He just ... treated me well. He was a good teacher. But about a week ago I saw something I wish I hadn't."

"What was that?"

"It was after school. I was studying for a while in the library, mostly waiting around for my friends to finish cheerleading practice. One of them said she'd give me a ride home. Seemed like they were taking forever. I decided to see if Mr. Fowler was still around. Talk to him about a homework assignment. I had a question. Well, maybe I just wanted to talk. In general, about stuff. He's a good listener. I mean was, I guess. Geez."

"Go on," I said, watching her carefully.

"So I went up to Mr. Fowler's office. The door was closed, and I knocked, but no answer. I heard something, so I figured he was inside. I opened the door, it was unlocked, and well, yeah. He was inside all right. No wonder he hadn't heard me knocking."

"Meaning?"

"Meaning," she said, her mouth becoming hard and her facial expression tightening. "Mr. Fowler was inside of Dash's mom, Skye. Deep inside, if you get what I'm saying."

# *Nine*

When I called the Pasadena police station, I received a stroke of luck; the person I was calling actually picked up. And adding to my good fortune, I learned he was working alone this weekend. I strolled into the near-empty station house and it took about a minute to find his desk. He sat there cleaning his weapon. He wore jeans and a black golf shirt, but he still looked decidedly average.

"Better make sure you've unloaded that thing, Detective," I said, pulling up a chair and sitting down, even though he hadn't invited me to join him. "Accidents do happen."

"I'll make sure it's pointed at a bad guy," said Al Diamond, displaying more character than I had given him credit for. "In case it misfires."

"Kind. Where's your partner?"

"Ah, Turco went up north this morning. Fishing trip. He stopped by before he left, to pick up some ammo."

"Ammo?" I asked, eyebrows up.

"Yeah. He brings a rod along. If the fish ain't biting, he uses his Beretta. Guess he doesn't want to go home empty-handed."

"Quite a sportsman, your partner."

"You get who you get," Diamond said with a yawn. "I've had better, I've had worse. Mostly better."

I smiled wistfully. Most of my partners on the job were very capable officers, but I suffered through a few who came with some jaw-dropping habits. From soliciting dates with attractive women we pulled over on routine traffic violations, to throwing a couple of sneaky punches on a manacled suspect, these partners pushed the envelope as far as the law would allow, and then kept going. One or two were dismissed after repeated charges were filed against them, but others continued on the job, surviving the occasional reprimand. Most had retired by now; once you put in your 20 years with the LAPD, the retirement benefits are generous. And due to a strong labor negotiation, the pension checks were an ironclad guarantee. The joke among the rank-and-file was that the checks would even be delivered to prison, if that's where a retired cop happened to wind up.

"How long have you been on the job?" I asked.

"Eighteen years," he said. "Would have been twenty, but I spent a couple of years with the Inglewood P.D. I live up in Lancaster, the drive was killing me. I like Pasadena better anyway. Nicer environment."

This was actually a little unusual. I knew cops who started out with the LAPD and left for nicer gigs like Thousand Oaks or Newport Beach, figuring their days would be more pleasant. It turned out their days were actually more boring, and most officers who enter law enforcement do so because it's interesting work. There's only so much job satisfaction one can garner by writing tickets for teenagers who were skateboarding illegally or shoplifting a six-pack of beer. The absence of a serious crime rate often sent those cops back to the LAPD. Time goes by faster when you're not suffering through terminal boredom at your job.

"Glad you're here on a weekend," I said.

"Had some paperwork and a few other things to take care of. So what brings you back? Planning to confess?"

"Nothing to confess to today," I said. "You crack the Jason Fowler case yet?"

"Nope. No suspects either. We've got some more work to do at that school. We'll be back there this week."

"Glad to hear you're giving yourself some space," I said dryly. "Maybe I can move things along a little quicker."

"Oh, yeah?" he asked, his attention suddenly becoming more focused. He put his weapon down on the desk. "What do you got?"

"I've got a lead that could turn you into a hero."

"Go on."

"I need something from you," I said.

"What do you think this is?" he sniffed. "*Let's Make A Deal*? C'mon. Out with it."

"I need help on a case."

"You and me both."

"So," I said, "if my lead pans out, I'd like some help trying to track down a check."

"A check?"

"Right. A large one. Maybe a few large ones. Drawn on Crown Bank. It's from the St. Dismas account, although it's probably set up as a charity or a foundation or something. That way the people who donate can write it off on their taxes. I was hired to track down what happened to over a hundred grand in missing funds. So any unusual activity in a St. Dismas account would be of great interest to me."

"Uh-huh. Okay, look. I'm not promising anything. If this lead pans out, then maybe we'll see."

"All right," I said, figuring this was likely the best I could hope for. "So I've been told Jason Fowler was having an affair."

Diamond snorted. "Guy wasn't married. Can't have an affair if you're not married. How does that work, smart guy?"

"It works," I said slowly, as if talking to a small child, "when the other person is married."

Diamond thought about this for a moment. "Okay. Who?"

"Her name's Skye Farsakian. Son goes to the school. Plays football. Again, this is just what I've been told. I wasn't there and I don't have much, other than hearsay. But right now, hearsay evidence is better than anything else you have. And it may actually be pretty solid."

Pulling out a folder, Diamond started combing through notes. "Yeah. Skye Farsakian. I interviewed her. Blonde, blue eyes, nice rack. Not bad for her age."

I frowned. "Why did you interview her?"

"She approached me. Right after the Fowler stabbing. I was talking with Mularkey, the principal, when she runs up. All distraught. Makes sense now. When you have a murder, everyone's on edge, but she was really upset. Didn't have anything concrete to say, only that the whole thing was horrible. We didn't think much of it at the time. Who would've thought she'd been getting banged by the dead guy. Makes sense now."

"You have a wonderful way with words, did you know that?" I said.

"Ah, lighten up. We'll talk to her again. If she had a kid at home, I imagine she and Fowler got a hotel room."

"Why do you say that?"

"Guy lived with his mom. Over thirty years old and still living at home. Fowler hadn't left the nest yet. Doubt he'd be bringing a married broad back to his mom's crib and then go do her in the bedroom he grew up in."

I took a breath. Diamond and Turco reminded me of why I didn't miss being a cop. "They did it in the school. On a desk in his office."

"No kidding. In a religious school? I'll be darned. Some people have no respect."

"Just don't say he got what was coming to him."

"I wasn't going to say it, but I was thinking it. How'd you learn about this?"

"A little bird told me."

Diamond sighed. "I'll need to talk with them."

I stopped and thought about this. I didn't like giving Vicki's name up, but realistically I had no reason to hide it. Maybe I could stonewall for a while. "I don't know as if I'm ready to pass a name along yet."

"Oh, you're not ready, huh?" Diamond said, his voice sounding annoyed. "So Fowler had a girlfriend. Girlfriend was older and married. They did it in a public place. Maybe they liked the thrill of living on the edge and not getting caught. Someone caught them. From all that, I can deduce two suspects. The girlfriend he was banging and the someone who walked in on them. You see why I need to talk with both, don't you?"

I looked down at the ground. I was pretty sure Vicki Sailor had nothing to do with Jason Fowler's death, but pretty sure wasn't good enough. I didn't know Vicki and couldn't rule her out. I did know what the police were going to put her through, though. It was fine if she were indeed the guilty party. If she were not, the episode would surely be humiliating for her. And it was all because she was forthcoming with me.

"All right," I sighed and wrote down her contact info. "I think you're going down the wrong path here, but I see your point. I assume you're going to get a DNA sample."

"Of course we are. How about this? A real-life P.I. who cooperates with the police. I ought to nominate you for an award or something."

"I'll settle for some help tracking down one of those checks."

*

As I began leaving Pasadena, I absently cruised past the stone building that housed St. Dismas High School, small shadows beginning to loom from the trees lining the perimeter of the campus. Next to the athletic facilities, I saw two vehicles in the parking lot. One was a silver

Mazda 3 with a bumper sticker indicating it was owned by a rental car chain. The other was a dark blue Ford Expedition, shiny and new. I parked next to the Ford, and noticed a small emblem stuck on the back window, one that told me who the owner was. The emblem featured a green shamrock and was embellished with the words *Fighting Irish*.

I sat in my Pathfinder, unsure of whether or not to enter the premises. I felt decidedly more comfortable going in if Duke Savich was alone, knowing I could handle him. But it looked like he had a visitor, and that represented a big unknown. Risking another altercation in a quiet building with the wrong people could have deadly consequences. After about three minutes, the situation resolved itself. Chuck Mantle walked out of the school and started to unlock his silver rental car.

"Hey there," I smiled, walking over. "Spending the weekend, I see. Doesn't that team of yours in Texas need you?"

"Well, looky here. If it isn't the Trojan warrior. Nah, we're on bye week. You still sniffing around this place?"

"Can't stay away," I said and shook his hand. "What'd you think of the game last night?"

"Learned some things," he said crisply.

"Don't need to worry about me stealing any intel. I'm out of that business."

"Sure you are. Until you're not. Look, we're still pursuing Noah, but maybe not as much now."

"Kid has some problems. They can be worked out. If he still wants to play football after this."

"I imagine he does. Savich told me he spoke with the parents. They said it was all an accident, no intentional overdose. Kid made an innocent mistake, that's all."

"Hope that's true," I said, doubting that it was.

"And we'll still offer him. Not too many kids come along with a cannon for an arm and a big brain, too. I can't say as if Noah'll take us up on it, every school in the nation is after him. But I'm tired of recruiting quarterbacks that can't get out of single digits on a Wonderlic test."

I shook my head. "Those tests don't mean much. Dan Marino had a low Wonderlic score. Wound up becoming one of the greatest QBs ever."

"Yeah, well, there are always outliers. Anyway, Noah has a big upside, but like I said, he just comes with some baggage."

"His father?" I asked, peering at him.

"His father, his mother, his coach. I just got done with Savich. There's another kid on the team I'm looking at. But Savich keeps pushing himself into the conversation and I finally had to tell him I'm recruiting players, not assistant coaches."

"How'd he take it?" I asked.

"How do you think he took it? Guy's desperate. You go to the game last night?"

"Yeah."

"Then you saw him. All over Noah whenever he made one false step. Savich has no control over his temper. I'm not bringing on a coach with an anger management problem. That guy is like a bull who brings along his own china shop."

I smiled. "Nice way to put it."

"Yeah, well the trip hasn't been a complete waste. I'm also offering that kid from De La Salle. The one who bull rushed past his guy and slammed Noah to the ground. Great effort. Man, that kid is a beast."

"He should have gotten called for a personal foul on that play. Helmet-to-helmet. Illegal hit."

"Maybe. But it doesn't hurt to have a badass or two on the team. I don't mind a guy who breaks the rules once in a while. Sometimes that's what it takes to win. Know what I mean?"

"Yeah," I said weakly, thinking I didn't want to look in the mirror right now. "I know exactly what you mean."

"Look, you know the drill. This is why we fly around the country. Nothing beats seeing players with your own two eyes, the film only tells you so much. One time we signed this *Parade* All-American, a center that was destroying everyone he faced. Never got to see him play in person, so we didn't know that his competition was mediocre. When we got the guy enrolled, we found out he could barely move our third-string nose guard out of the way."

"I know. I remember the life."

"All right. Well, good luck to you. Let me know if you ever want to get back into this world," Mantle said, opening the car door. "And by the way, I hear you're not a guy to mess with."

I stared at him. "How'd you hear that?"

"Word gets around. Underwood told me, actually. Don't worry. Savich isn't filing charges. Coaches live and die by their image as tough guys. Hard to do that if everyone knows you got punched out by someone. Doesn't matter by who."

I took this in and gave a quick wave to Mantle as he got in his car and barreled out of the parking lot. Taking a deep breath, I walked inside the building, down the narrow hall. I cast a shadow over Duke Savich's doorway. He was sitting at his desk, looking down at some papers. I rapped softly. He glanced at me and then jumped up and pointed a finger.

"What the hell are you doing here?" Savich demanded.

"Only want to talk," I said, raising my hands. "I come in peace."

Savich reached across his desk, grabbed a knife and held it up, gripping it in more of a defensive posture than in a menacing way. But his eyes were wide and he had that crazed look a person gets when they're scared. It's a look which communicates the person is capable of anything, and they are not rational enough to think deeply about the consequences of their actions.

"Get out of here!" he barked.

I looked over at a metal chair in the corner and sat down. Reaching down, I placed my right hand on my ankle holster. Just in case. I gave him a bored look.

"Sit down and put that knife away," I said softly. "I'm not looking for a brawl. But if you come at me, I'm going to shoot you. I don't want to shoot you. I've got better things to do tonight than spend it explaining to the police why I had to shoot you."

He stood there for a long moment before sanity began to wash over him. It took some time, but he finally seemed to realize just how foolish he looked. He tossed the knife on the desk, and then sheepishly sat down and slid back in his chair.

"All right. Just what the hell do you want now?" he asked in a voice that was tinged with fatigue.

I pointed to his desk. "You always keep a knife nearby? Is Pasadena that tough a place these days?"

"Smartass. We use it to scrape the dried mud off of the cleats. Why else would we need it?"

"I don't know," I lied. "Why would you have mud stuck on players' cleats in the first place? We haven't had rain here in six months."

"Sprinkler system," he shrugged. "Someone fiddled with the timer. Goes off five times a day some days. Been happening for a while, I just can't get it stopped. And the Department of Water and Power is now saying we're liable for a big fine if we don't fix it soon. They say we're wasting water."

"Uh-huh," I said and tried to steer him back to a more prescient matter. "Anyone else have access to that knife?"

"Just what the hell are you implying?" he asked, his indignation starting to rise.

"What else? Jason Fowler."

He stared at me. "That's crazy. And no. Only the coaches and the team manager. Why the hell would anyone around here want to stab a teacher?"

"Someone did."

"Yeah, well, I can't imagine who. Had to have been an outsider. Unrelated to the team."

"All right," I said.

"That it? Anything else you want to accuse me of?"

"Maybe. I'm still looking into where all the fundraising money went."

Savich sighed. "Here and there. Earl should mind his own damned business."

"He's not going to. And at this point, neither am I. This is sounding more and more like fraud."

"You don't know what you're talking about. It actually has to do with that sprinkler system."

"The one that's broken and you haven't spent the money to fix?" I asked. "I guess that's cheaper than installing field turf."

"Couple of kids got hurt. Parents sued. We're paying their medical bills. Not something we want to fund out of the school coffers."

"Why not? Doesn't the school have insurance?"

"It's an out-of-court settlement. Plus, we need to keep it quiet. We still have to recruit new kids every year. Bad publicity for a school that has more than its share of kids getting injured."

"That's where over a hundred thousand dollars went?" I asked skeptically.

"I'm not going to discuss everything with you. I don't care if you have a gun or not. Some things are off limits."

"Earl's not going to stop poking here."

"Tell Earl to go fuck himself. I'm tired of his shit. Tired of a lot of things around here. Last night was so bad. National exposure against De La Salle. And we blew it."

I looked at Savich slumping in his chair. He struck me as a man who was running out of options. And once Noah signed, all of his leverage would be gone.

"Tell me about Skye Farsakian," I said, trying to keep him focused on the subject at hand.

"Skye? What about her? She's a team parent. Helps out."

"She was involved with Jason Fowler."

Savich's eyebrows lifted. "What do you mean?"

"I know she's been raising more than just funds."

Savich glared at me. "You've got a dirty mind."

"I wasn't the one who made reference to the size of her breasts. What's her involvement in all of this? I'm going to find out anyway. Why don't you just tell me."

"Skye helps out. It's good for us and good for her. She's had it rough. Her husband left her last year, now he's wants back in. That poor woman's got to be confused as hell."

"So you figure that's why Skye was having an affair with Fowler," I said, watching him closely. His eyes narrowed and his breathing became erratic. I took a quick glance at his desk to be certain where the knife was.

"Really, I don't know what you're talking about," he said. "That's news to me. But if you're implying Skye Farsakian had some involvement in Fowler's murder, you're nuts. Skye couldn't hurt an ant."

I got up. "So what's the future hold for you?"

"I don't know," Savich said. "Tonight I'm going to curl up with a bottle of Bushmills and try to drink this weekend away."

I didn't blame him. But I felt like telling him you couldn't drown your problems because they just learn to swim. Instead, I left without saying anything more because I doubted he'd pay any attention. I got in the Pathfinder and headed back to Mar Vista. On the way, I called up Al Diamond and told him about a knife sitting on the desk in Duke Savich's office.

## *Ten*

The Pasadena heat had finally drifted over to the Westside, and by 9:00 a.m. on Sunday morning, Mar Vista had reached 81 degrees. Gail and I decided this would make for an excellent beach day, provided we got to Santa Monica quickly. If we arrived early enough, we'd have our pick of beaches. But people tend to go back to where they know, the familiar terrain, and in L.A. that often means a place where you know you can secure a parking spot.

The small lots next to the main beach were already full, so I drove up the California Incline and parked along the bluffs at Ocean and Montana. This was only a few blocks from where we used to live, back in the days when we were unencumbered, which was another way of saying childless. It was also where Rebecca Linzmeier still lived. Walking down the steps to the sand, I had the feeling that Marcus, excited as he was at the prospect of splashing around in the ocean, would probably need to be carried back up once his energy abated. I didn't relish the thought of it, but it was a responsibility that came along with being a dad. The joys, however, of seeing Marcus grow, and appreciating the wonders of childhood, were things that more than offset any inconvenience.

We settled in and I led Marcus down to the water's edge. The surf was mild today, and we played a game of running toward the ocean until the wave was about to break. As the water slid quickly toward us, we darted back toward the warm sand. Occasionally, the wave would wash over our feet, and Marcus would giggle excitedly as the cold water raced under him. We played catch with a very soft mini-football, and I encouraged him to catch it with his hands and then nestle it against his body. Once in a while he succeeded, and I gave him a big round of applause. We eventually made our way back to Gail, and she set Marcus up with a pail of wet sand and let him begin making a castle. I collapsed into a beach chair and pulled out a Coke from the cooler.

"Mmmm," I sighed, closing my eyes as I took a sip. "That tastes better than you can imagine."

"You've had a long week," Gail said. "I hope Earl is paying you overtime."

"I got a four-day retainer, but I've blown past that. The investigation has sailed beyond merely embezzling funds, it's now murder. I don't know that I can charge Earl for looking into that, too."

"Will the murder investigation help lead you to where the missing funds went?"

I thought about that. "Maybe. I'm working an angle."

"Then it sounds like you've got a reasonable argument."

"If he'll cough up this time. I don't care to wait another eight years for payment."

Gail smiled. She was wearing a black one-piece bathing suit and looked good. She always looked good. Her brown hair was pulled back in a ponytail, and she was busy squirting sunscreen into her hand and rubbing it onto Marcus's back as he worked diligently on his project.

"People can evolve."

"Sometimes. I'll show you the extra check if I get it. You'll need to help me spend it."

"I can work with that," she smiled. "So we've barely had time to talk this week. How are things going on this case?"

I took another long pull on the can of Coke and looked out at the distant horizon. It was a perfect horizon. The ocean was a dark blue, almost purplish in fact, and there were no clouds in the sky. The forecast was for Santa Monica to reach the high 80s, which meant most everywhere else would be in the high 90s at least. I imagined Pasadena would surely hit triple digits.

"Things are going quite slowly," I sighed.

"What have you uncovered so far?" Gail asked.

"There's a woman who has a role in both of these events, although it may be peripheral. Her name is Skye Farsakian."

"Now that's quite a name."

"Yeah. She was the parent helping to chair the fundraising drive for the football program. But she doesn't seem to have played any part in where the money went after that."

"And how is she connected to the murder?"

"She was sleeping with the victim," I said.

"Ah. The plot thickens. A team parent having an affair with a teacher."

"Not quite what it seems. Her husband left her for a younger woman. They were separated. Nothing ostensibly wrong with her having a fling, although doing the deed in the teacher's office wasn't using good judgment."

"How did you find out about this?" she frowned.

"One student told me he was walking by the office one day and heard it. Might or might not have meant anything, but a second student said she actually walked in on them. In the act. She sounded honest. Didn't seem like she played any role in this other than as a brief and unintended observer."

"Did either student tell the police?"

"No, I doubt they understood the implications of all this."

"Ouch."

"Teenagers," I reminded her. "Probably don't plan to go into law enforcement."

"It's not a career for everyone," Gail said and reached into the cooler to pull out a Coke for herself.

"And then there's this guy named Noah Greenland, who's got a national reputation."

"Principal?"

"Quarterback. He's one of the most sought-after recruits in the nation. Johnny got him to commit to SC last year, but Noah decommitted when Johnny left for Chicago. Seems like everyone wants to grab a piece of this kid's success. He's having a bad time of it, and senior year in high school is one period where you're supposed to enjoy yourself."

"How is he related to this case?"

"I don't know. Maybe he isn't. His father used to coach at St. Dismas. But Noah played poorly in Friday night's game. Then he went home and swallowed a bottle of sleeping pills."

"He obviously has more problems than simply having a bad game."

"May have been an accident. But something's not right there. I'd say he needs to see a psychologist, but he already has one in the family, his mother. And his father not only was the former coach, but he got fired from the school to boot. It's complicated."

"Quite a combination he has for parents, a therapist and a football coach."

"I guess. Sometimes an odd combination works. In this case, not so much. I thought I'd seen it all. But I'd never had a parent blatantly ask for cash to get their son to commit to a college. That's apparently what his father was doing."

Gail sighed. "Parents these days are becoming more like career managers, not the traditional moms and dads of the past. And those are the ones who technically operate within the law. My goodness. I just finished prosecuting a father-son burglary team."

"Don't see that every day," I said.

"No. Apparently the father would go to one of the long-term parking lots near the airport. He'd break into the cars, but he was only after two things. The owner's address, and their garage-door opener. Then he'd give both to the son."

"Ah. Bonding through crime. So the son didn't have to worry about picking the front-door lock."

"Exactly. They knew the people were traveling and unlikely to be home, so the son would go and burglarize the house."

I had heard about this trick many years ago. "And since the victims weren't congregated in one neighborhood, the police didn't notice a pattern."

"Yes. Some of the victims posted vacation pictures on Facebook, but not everyone did. It all seemed random."

"How did they end up getting caught?"

"One of the houses they broke into. Turns out the wife was on a business trip, but the husband was home. And he had a .44 lying around. He heard the garage door open, and when the son started to enter, well, he got a nasty surprise. He got shot in the foot."

"Not a good day for him. Did the police get him to turn in his father?" I asked.

"No, the homeowner did. Shot him in the other foot and said he'd keep shooting until he told him how he got ahold of the garage door opener. He gave his father up pretty quick."

"I guess police interrogations have their limitations," I said with a smile. "The private sector can be more efficient in this area."

Gail rolled her eyes. "We have to live by a set of rules in society. We can't have people taking the law into their own hands."

"Don't tell me you're prosecuting the homeowner for protecting his property?"

"No. The City Attorney's planning a run for Mayor next cycle. Wouldn't be good politics to go after a burglary victim, regardless of whether he was recklessly disregarding the law. Or whether he was engaging in torture."

"I doubt the burglars will file a civil suit."

"They're both looking at five-to-ten in San Quentin. They have larger issues on their plates."

At that point, Marcus walked over to us. "Mommy," he started, putting his pail on the sand.

"Yes, Marcus?" Gail asked.

"I have a question."

"Go ahead, sweetheart."

"What's torture mean?" he asked, eyes wide and innocent.

I looked at Gail. She turned and looked back at me. I glanced back out at the distant horizon. It did not seem so perfect any longer.

\*

After spending the better part of our Sunday at the beach, I did indeed have to carry Marcus up the narrow path along the palisade bluffs. And though Gail managed to slather him generously with sunscreen, she somehow forgot to do the tops of his feet, which were now very pink. Some aloe gel helped with the pain, and a barbecued hot dog seemed to divert his attention, at least for a little while. I grilled burgers for Gail and myself, and we ended what was largely a nice day, even though there was a brief interlude where we both stumbled valiantly through an extremely vague and sugar-coated definition of torture.

I slept long into Monday morning, somehow dozing through whatever activity the jets at Santa Monica Airport were engaged in. I was planning to go to Pasadena, but there was no need to get there early. In fact, no need to get there prior to the start of football practice. I stopped by my office, did some paperwork, and right before I was about to leave, fielded a call from Rebecca Linzmeier. She informed me her boyfriend had set up yet another dinner tomorrow night, and she wanted me to conduct another stakeout. This time she wanted to find out what room her boyfriend would be in. I started to regret offering her a sliding scale.

"I want to catch him in the act," she said.

Once again, I cautioned her against doing so, but she was resolute. And I finally acknowledged that a peaceful confrontation might be the only way to get closure here. I asked if she owned a gun and she said no. I asked if she could control herself enough to prevent this from unfolding into a melee worthy of a *Jerry Springer* segment. There was a long silence followed by a meek objection, but I was firm in my position. This was the only way I'd help her. She agreed, but I thought I heard a gulp on the other end of the line. I told her I'd accompany her, and I insisted she only use her words and absolutely nothing else. As I drove up to Pasadena, I replayed the conversation in my mind. I couldn't escape the unsettled feeling that I had been speaking to a grossly immature woman whose emotional barometer was approaching that of a small child. Marcus struck me as having more control over himself than did Rebecca Linzmeier. She was only about 35 years older than he was.

The St. Dismas players were already lined up on the field, stretching and getting ready for practice. I climbed up the bleachers and took a seat by myself. The atmosphere was quiet and subdued, as was often the case following a tough loss. There were a few people watching from the stands, but they struck me as parents, not college scouts. Duke Savich tried to provide a spark, but the players were only going through the motions. There was little energy. And when they lined up to scrimmage, I noticed a player wearing number 19 had taken his place over the center, barking signals. Austin Bainbridge was the new quarterback. I heard someone a few rows below me yell out encouragement. Looking down, I saw Dash Farsakian's husky frame draped over two rows, wearing a green t-shirt and watching the practice, a can of Arizona Iced Tea in his hand. I climbed down and sat next to him.

"Not practicing today?" I asked.

"Oh, hi," Dash replied and then shook his head. "Sprained my ankle at the end of the De La Salle game."

"Tough loss."

"Yeah. I feel terrible. The player that knocked out Noah was my guy. I missed the block. I thought he was going to take an outside route, but when I slid that way, he spun inside, and my ankle gave out. Guy had a super quick first step. Noah didn't stand a chance back there."

"You were battling him pretty good most of the way. I was there, I saw it. You have nothing to be ashamed about."

"I guess. But I know there were some big-name college scouts in the crowd. Bad time to miss a key block. You wouldn't happen to still have some pull with the SC coaches?"

I shook my head. "Different regime, sorry. But try not to beat yourself up over it. You're good enough to get a scholarship somewhere. And trust me, not everyone playing in the NFL comes out of an elite college program. Plenty of them went to mid-majors."

"Yeah," he said blankly.

"Best thing you can do is try and forget about that missed block," I said, knowing it was unlikely. This was the type of mistake a good player would replay a hundred times in his head, trying to make the result come out differently. It's a team game, but sometimes a game turns on one play, and that hit to Noah was the one.

"It's hard to do," he sighed.

"Sure. Too bad that your ankle gave out at the wrong time."

"Actually, I had tweaked it last week in practice. Was doing okay with it until that play. Doc says to stay off it for a few days."

I looked out onto the field. The grass seemed wet and slick. "Lot of practice injuries here?"

"Yeah. I don't know what the deal is with the sprinklers. Some days it's like a swamp out there. We've lost a number of guys in practice. They say injuries are a part of the game, but it's tough. You lose a guy who's a big part of the team and it changes everything. I know about this next man up thing, but it doesn't always work. And losing Noah on Friday was critical. I love Austin, but Noah was special."

"Will Noah be back?" I asked.

"I dunno. His mother doesn't want him to. But she never wanted him to play in the first place. Man, dealing with parents sucks. Mine are either breaking up or getting back together."

I took a breath. "How well are you acquainted with Noah?"

"I've only known Noah a couple of years. But there's something that's always been different about him. On the field, he's like this robo-quarterback, perfect in so many ways. He rarely makes a mistake. When he does, if he overthrows a receiver or something, he's tougher on himself than anyone. That's why a lot of the guys hate Savich. When we screw up, Savich is all over us. That doesn't work with Noah. A player like that needs a different kind of coach. Coach Curly seemed to be able to get through to him better."

"Pretty astute observation."

"I guess."

"So how do you think Austin will do as quarterback?"

Dash shrugged. "Okay. I hope he does well. It's what he's always wanted. Austin has a good arm. But he has hasn't played quarterback in two years. And I don't know how the team will respond. Once you play with a guy like

Noah, you see how far he can throw, that rocket arm and all. It's difficult to get behind anyone else."

"Mmm-hmmm," I agreed. "No doubt. Quarterback's the most important position on the field. Have you heard if Noah is out of the hospital?"

"Not yet. I saw him yesterday, they finally started allowing visitors in. He'll be all right. They got him to the E.R. quick. He's a little shaken up, but physically he'll be okay."

"Did you notice anything odd about Noah's behavior last week?" I asked. "Anything that could explain why he did it?"

"Yeah, something was weird. He seemed worried during the game on Friday. Real nervous and stuff."

"What do you see?"

"He was tentative. Even in warm-ups. Maybe all the pregame hype, the TV cameras. Then the game started, and he really didn't have it. Didn't go through his progressions. But every now and then you'd see the real Noah. He'd drill a throw. Squeeze it right into that little window quarterbacks talk about. Then he'd get distracted about something. I guess anyone can have a bad game. But I've never seen it happen to Noah."

"Anything going on with him outside of school?" I asked.

Dash shrugged again. "I dunno."

I heard a noise behind the bleachers. It sounded like a gasp at first, maybe a moan. I looked down but didn't see anything. Then there was more moaning, followed by the rasp of someone cursing. Dash and I looked at each other, puzzled. Then out of the corner of my eye, I saw a blur, the movement of someone racing out from under the bleachers. It was the team's equipment manager, Colin Holder. He tore around the corner of the bleachers, out of breath and hunched over.

"What's the matter, Colin?" Dash yelled.

"Someone call 9-1-1. Now! This guy's on the ground. He ain't moving, he's bleeding!"

We both got up, but I was the one with the good legs, so I ran quickly down and around the bleachers until I reached the underside. I saw a man lying on the ground, face down in the wet grass. Blood was all over the place. One feature jumped out at me. There was no mistaking the shiny, sunburned head. I rolled the man over and shook him hard, but he didn't move. I checked his pulse, but there was none. Bob Greenland's eyes were open, but it was an empty and vacuous look that stared back at me. His throat had been cut and there was blood all over his upper torso. There was no need to call paramedics. It looked like he had been dead for a while.

## *Eleven*

It was, to quote a famous man, *deja vu* all over again. Medical trucks, police cruisers, and news vans lined the street outside St. Dismas High School. The Pasadena police instructed all the players to stay on the practice field and not leave the area until the detectives had interviewed them. Duke Savich tried to protest that his players knew nothing about this, but Al Diamond quickly, and rather emphatically, told him to shut up or the coach would give his statement in handcuffs down at the station.

Most of the players sat down quietly and patiently on the grass. The detectives were methodical but thorough. And though it took a little while, Hugh Turco finally made his way over to me, bringing his acerbic wit along with him. As much as I had wished to be interviewed by his partner, lady luck was not on my side today. Al Diamond was off interviewing someone else.

"Well, I guess I shouldn't be too surprised," Turco said. "You're one of the first ones to find the body. Just happen to have the knack of being in the wrong place at the wrong time, eh Burnside?"

"Some guys have the gift," I said. "How was your fishing trip? Shoot any bass? My guess is they were moving too quickly for you. Maybe you should have brought along an assault rifle."

"Still the smart aleck. Okay. Why don't you give me your story here. Or your alibi. Whatever's easier for you to make up."

I told him every relevant thing I had seen and done at St. Dismas today, which took barely more than thirty seconds. Turco made a motion with his fingers indicating he wanted something additional.

"That's all there is," I said, raising my palms skyward, knowing that too many smart remarks would earn me another trip to the police station. "I was talking with one of the players in the stands. The equipment manager came running over and he was yelling. I went under the stands and found the body."

"You know this guy, this Bob Greenland?"

"I talked with him once. Recently. During the football game last Friday night. Can't say we had a deep conversation. Nothing that would lead me to believe someone would kill him. Frankly, I thought he'd get a heart attack first."

"Oh, yeah?"

"His son plays for the team. Maybe you've heard of him. Noah Greenland?"

Turco shook his head. "Not before last week's shooting over here. I got better things to do than waste my time watching football. Stupid game."

"I imagine it can be hard to follow," I said, noticing Turco's eyes narrowing, and then hastened to add, "if you aren't familiar with the rules and all."

"Yeah," he responded slowly. "So who was this Bob Greenland mad at? His son? The other team?"

"He was ticked at pretty much everyone. But he had a few choice words for the coach. Didn't like the plays he was calling."

"Uh-huh. The coach is that Savich guy? The one who got annoyed that a murder investigation was interfering with his practice?"

"One and the same," I said.

"We'll give him a good grilling later. So tell me more about the dead guy."

"Bob."

"Huh?"

"His name was Bob. Bob Greenland," I said, figuring at the very least, Noah's father could get the courtesy of being referred to as something other than 'the dead guy.'

"Yeah, yeah. What else do you know about him?"

"Used to be a coach here. A few years back. He got fired. Apparently he had a run-in with a parent. Some dad got mouthy with him and Bob tossed the guy through a door."

"Sounds like a tough *hombre*," Turco mused.

"I suppose. But he lost his job because of it."

"And maybe that dad has a long memory," Turco said. "Got a name?"

I thought for a moment. "Pretty sure it was Stan Weekes. One of the parents could confirm it. Don't know much more."

"We'll check him out. What about the kid. This Noah. Think there's anything there?"

I looked at him oddly. "You think Noah had something to do with his father getting killed?"

"Wouldn't be the first time."

"No," I said, thinking back to a case I worked on some years ago, where a son shot his father to death in cold blood. But that was unique in many ways, including the fact that the guy pulling the trigger made his living as a paid assassin.

"This Noah get along with his dad?" Turco asked.

"Don't know them well enough," I said. "Like I told you, I only spoke to the dad once, and that was brief. Same with the son. The kid obviously had problems. But this? I don't know. Hard to figure."

"Got to ask," Turco said. "You know the drill."

"There's something else," I added reluctantly.

"What?" he asked.

"I don't know the relevance here, but I heard Bob was hitting on one of the other player's moms. Name's Talley Kingston. As you might imagine, her husband wasn't pleased."

Turco's head bobbed up and down excitedly at this news. "I like that. What's the name of the husband?"

"Buzz," I said. "Buzz Kingston."

"Okay," Turco said, jotting it down on a pad of paper. "Now we're getting somewhere. I like it when P.I.'s cooperate."

"Look, I don't know what might come of this. Talley Kingston said she turned Bob down flat."

"Well, it's something to go on anyway," he said.

"Sure," I said. One clue often leads to another, and then another. If you gather enough of them, you can sometimes piece things together. That is, if you know what you're doing, and I was doubting Turco would have the necessary diligence or brainpower to unravel this puzzle. But withholding information from the police was not always advisable, and could even cost me my license, so it was often better to share.

"I heard you tried to help us out the other day," he said.

"Just doing my civic duty."

"Nice of you. But too bad that blade Savich had didn't match up. Would have made things easy for us, knife sitting right in the coach's office. Our forensics guys said this wasn't the weapon that killed Fowler."

"Pretty fast determination. They run DNA testing that quick?" I asked. While some DNA evidence could be determined in a few hours, most required at least a week. And given the backup in most labs, it was not uncommon to take a few weeks. Or longer.

"Nah. They did it the old-fashioned way. The blade that killed Fowler was serrated. The knife in the coach's office was a straight blade. Actually, I'd be surprised if that knife Savich had could even cut a salami, it was so dull. Blind alley, Burnside. Do better next time."

"Worth a shot," I said and then looked around to see where Dash was. He was still sitting over in the bleachers, well beyond hearing distance. "You interview Vicki Sailor?"

"Of course we interviewed her," Turco sniffed. "Her story makes no sense. She said she walked in on Fowler doing the nasty on his desk. Yeah, maybe Fowler was banging someone, but an old broad like that? That Skye's got to be 45, at least. With all this young stuff running around here? C'mon. I think this Vicki Sailor may be making the whole thing up. She's on our radar."

"Meaning?" I frowned.

"We know she had a thing for Fowler. Used to go up to his office a lot to chat. Or whatever. Maybe she did see him with someone else, who knows. Maybe that set off something in her. Yeah, Vicki Sailor's story about Skye matched up with what she told you. Doesn't mean it was the truth. Or made any sense."

Nothing about Vicki Sailor had set off any warning bells with me. While I wasn't always perfect at reading people, I had at least become pretty good. Most of the time. But standard police protocol was to treat everyone as a suspect and view their stories through a jaundiced eye. I had a bad feeling about this. Sometimes people are indeed lying, and good detectives have a radar for it. They need to be able to get suspects and witnesses to feel comfortable enough to open up in front of them. This could be a difficult art for detectives like Turco, who came slathered in a thick coat of people-repellant.

"I hope you have a little more to go on than just this," I managed.

"We're working it," he said. "We found something of hers in Fowler's office. She was doing her teacher, no doubt in my mind."

"Oh?"

"Yeah, can't talk about it yet. But we're on to something. Murder and sex. The two sure seem to go together," Turco said.

As he proceeded to prattle on about how smart he was, one of the medical examiners came over and whispered something into Turco's ear. He bobbed his head up and down enthusiastically, told the medico he was doing good work, and patted him on the back.

"Crack the case?" I asked.

"Man, oh, man," he bellowed. "It's unbelievable what our guys do! These M.E. techs, they think of everything. The stiff isn't even in the morgue yet, but these guys have the presence of mind to check him out."

"What did they check out?" I peered at him.

"Looks like this Greenland was getting his pud wet this afternoon. Right behind the bleachers. Geez, is everyone at this school getting their ashes hauled on campus?"

"Charming language."

"Ah, don't rain on my parade. The M.E. techs found stains on Bob Greenland's drawers. Someone had a little afternoon delight with him. Then decided to slit his throat. Won't be hard to see if there's a DNA match with Vicki Sailor. I think we're dealing with a black widow spider here. I'll bet she did Fowler, too. Looks like we're gettin' close to the finish line."

\*

I decided against returning to Pasadena the next day. The police would take a dim view of my showing up at St. Dismas, and I could not imagine I'd be granted access to the campus. And perhaps as importantly, the school had a clear need to mourn. Capital crimes have been occurring on high school campuses more frequently these days, but it was almost unimaginable that a school would have to go through this nightmare twice in less than a week. The tragedy of having a teacher murdered on school grounds, regardless of the reason, followed by the murder of a parent soon after, was a jarring and frightening situation. Even in today's hardened media world, teenagers are still impressionable, and the blinding spotlight of the national press could be almost as overwhelming as the incidents themselves. And staying away would also let me focus on my other case.

It was right before 5:30 p.m. when I pulled up at Shutters Hotel, and I handed the neatly dressed valet the keys to my Pathfinder. I knew I was an hour ahead of Doug Trueblood's scheduled arrival, but I wanted to become more familiar with the surroundings. I rode the elevator up to a few of the floors, and they looked identical. The hallways were spacious, the decor was beautiful, and the carpeting was plush. I found the emergency stairwells in the event I needed to use them. I noticed a door open in one of the guest rooms and a housekeeper was in the midst of cleaning the room. I strolled in, looked around, then effusively apologized for entering the wrong room. It was a nice room, large, but no different than any other nice hotel, except that these windows looked out onto a panoramic view of Santa Monica Bay, the glistening Pacific shimmering under a late afternoon sun.

Back down into the lobby, I seated myself in a comfy chair facing the front door. There was the usual pre-dinner activity, and a few other people were seated nearby, either chatting with a companion or awaiting one. People came, people went. Finally, after about 45 minutes, Doug Trueblood sauntered in. I watched him carefully and was ready to get up and follow him. But he didn't head toward the elevator this time. Instead, he scanned the lobby, a quizzical expression on his face. Then he smiled knowingly and walked over to a young woman seated about 20 feet away.

It was an understatement to say she was young and beautiful. She was also tall and had a shapely figure. Her golden blonde hair cascaded halfway down her back. She had sparkling green eyes, drawn out by a low-cut Kelly-green top and a gold necklace. She wore white slacks and managed to pull off the difficult trick of looking both elegant and casual at the same time. And to my keenly trained investigator's mind, she looked as if she were all of, but no more than, twenty-one years old.

She stood up and they embraced. They gazed into each other's eyes. He smiled and she smiled. I decided to wait until they turned toward the elevator before following them, my goal being to avoid the hint of suspicion it might bring. But they did not journey to the elevator and up to one of the hotel rooms. Instead, they walked across the lobby and up the short set of stairs into the dining room. I slowly followed, maintaining a good distance before stopping at the entrance.

After they were seated at a table facing the ocean, I walked into the spacious restaurant and headed toward the bar. It was an impressive room. The vaulted, highbeam ceiling was painted white, and there were black wrought-iron light fixtures hanging down over each table. The hardwood floors positively gleamed. Easing onto a stool, I picked up a menu and scanned it absently. Everything looked sublimely interesting and extraordinarily expensive. This was the type of place I might have taken Gail when I was making a robust income as a football coach, and paying for a babysitter was easy. These days, date night was more likely to be dinner at The Cheesecake Factory, and occasionally we would include Marcus. I set the menu down on the bar and ordered a passion fruit iced tea. The young, overly-friendly bartender smiled brightly and told me today was his first day on the job. He tried to be chatty, but I just smiled and looked the other way. After he moved on down the bar, I pulled out my phone.

Rebecca Linzmeier answered on the first ring and dispensed with any hint of formality or greeting. It was strictly business at this point.

"Are you there?" she said almost breathlessly.

"I'm here," I answered.

"What room are they doing it in?"

"They're not doing it in a room."

"What are you talking about?! What are they ... doing it in public?!"

I sighed. "Don't be ridiculous. And calm down."

"You calm down," she snarled. "My life is falling apart. Tell me what's going on."

"They're having dinner," I said. "In the hotel dining room."

"Shutters?"

"Yes, Shutters."

"I'll be right there."

"Rebecca."

"Yes."

"Remember our agreement," I said.

There was a long pause and then the line went dead. I shook my head and put my phone back in my pocket. I double-checked my ankle holster and took a long drink of iced tea. I briefly thought of ordering a shot of Jack Daniels, but decided that would have to wait. I tried to avoid staring at Doug Trueblood and his companion, occasionally shooting a glance their way to make sure they hadn't left, without making it seem obvious that I was spying. Or leering. I didn't know how Doug Trueblood came to know a girl like this, but she was impressive. He might indeed be committing infidelity, a show-stopping violation of his relationship, but I couldn't prevent myself from considering the fact that the man seemed to have remarkably good taste.

Rebecca Linzemeier appeared at the entrance of the restaurant and spoke briefly to the maître d'. He waved her on in, and I slipped off my barstool and hurried to intercept her. I moved directly into her path and put out my hands.

"What are you doing?" she demanded.

"Trying to keep things civil."

"I need to confront him. He's right there. I see what he's doing."

"Don't make a scene," I said, adding an admonishment I would occasionally employ with Marcus. "Remember, you promised."

She took a breath. "All right."

"I'll be right behind you," I said, wondering if I should also remind her to use her inside voice. "But I'm not afraid to jerk you away if I see even the hint of anything ugly about to happen."

"All *right*," she snapped.

Rebecca pushed past me and approached the couple. They had just finished their appetizer. It looked as if he had ordered the fried calamari and she had had the kale salad. I wondered if they were worth $18 apiece.

"Doug," Rebecca started, her voice dripping with sarcasm. "So nice to see you here. I hope your business meeting is going well."

"Sweetheart," he said, putting his napkin on the table and getting up. "I wasn't expecting you."

"I'm sure you weren't," she said, her voice beginning to crack and her hands balling up into small fists.

"Why are you here?" he asked.

"Why do you think?" she responded and began eyeing the young woman. At that point, I stepped forward and placed myself in-between Rebecca and the couple.

"Hello there," I said with a smile. "I'm Burnside."

Doug Trueblood reached over and shook my hand. "You look familiar."

"I get that a lot."

"You used to live in Rebecca's building."

"I did. About three years ago. Good memory."

"Where are you now?"

"Over in Mar Vista. We bought a house."

"I hear that's a nice area."

"Yeah, we like it."

"Jesus H. Christ!" exploded Rebecca. "Are you two going to be best buds now?! I want to know what the hell's going on here! Who *is* this woman, Doug?!"

"Sweetheart, look ..."

"Is this how it ends? After six years in a relationship? This is what happens?"

The beautiful young woman tried to speak. "I don't think you quite understand. It's really ... "

"Really what?!" Rebecca screamed, some tears starting to stream down her face, as people at other tables turned to watch the spectacle. "Tell me what it really is?"

"Sweetheart, I didn't know how to explain it to you," Doug said.

"You could have been a man and just said so," she sobbed. "You didn't have to run around behind my back."

"I'm not," he pleaded. "Honest, I'm not. I want to explain."

I put my hand on Rebecca's arm. "Let him speak."

"This isn't some girlfriend," he said, raising his hands for emphasis. "She's much more than that."

Rebecca stared. "More?!"

"It's ... well ... "

"I'm his daughter," the beautiful young woman broke in. "One he didn't know he had until a few months ago."

"What?"

"Yes," the young woman said with a sad smile. "I looked him up. In fact, I went and hired a private detective to find him. I always wanted to find my birth parents. To find out about who they were. To find out about who I am."

The expression on Rebecca Linzmeier's face was a mixture of shock and disbelief. She brushed away the tears, and for a moment I thought I saw her face relax. "That's just ... so ... I had no idea."

"I was adopted," she continued. "Dad said they had me when they were very young, didn't think they were ready to be parents."

"We weren't even ready to be married," Doug added. "We broke up a few months later."

I took a glance around the dining room. A few patrons were still staring, but most had gone back to their meals, the drama having been alleviated as far as they needed it to be. I cleared my throat. "Were your adopted parents wealthy by chance?" I asked.

"Oh, no. Middle-class. Wonderful people, but not rich. They were insurance agents, actually. We had a nice house, but nothing fancy."

"So then how'd you wind up staying at Shutters?" I asked, sensing this was none of my business, but curiosity was an ingrained trait I would never shed.

"I'm an actress," she smiled. "I landed a part in a TV series. They fly me out here to L.A. a lot when we're shooting. The studio puts me up. The side benefit is I get to see Dad."

I looked over at Rebecca and she was still blinking away tears, but they no longer seemed like tears of rage. She fell into Doug's arms and hugged him for a long time. I sensed this would be a good time for me to exit, as my work here was done. I gave everyone a little wave and headed for the door. As I quickly walked down the stairs, the young, overly-friendly bartender came flying after me. He did not look so friendly any more.

"Sir!"

I turned back to him. "Yes?"

"Are you going to pay for your drink?"

I gave him a blank stare. I had forgotten all about that.

"I don't want to have to call the police," he said sternly.

"No," I said, reaching into my wallet and wondering how much the police would laugh if they were called about a petty matter like this. "I wouldn't want you to call the police. And I doubt the manager of this hotel would want you to, either."

# Twelve

I spent the better part of the next few days basking in the glow of a closed case. There was no betrayal and no cheating, and the tears of rage managed to evolve into tears of joy. The only thing that could have upended Rebecca Linzmeier's relationship with a good man was Ms. Linzmeier herself. Fortunately, she caught herself in time, and I liked to think I played a role, small perhaps, but undeniably necessary. Had I not been around, Rebecca might well have thrown a drink at her boyfriend before either he or his daughter could explain things.

The few messages I left for the detectives in Pasadena yielded not even the courtesy of a returned phone call. It was hardly a surprise, detectives are often busy, and keeping a lowly P.I. in the loop is relegated to the bottom of their to-do list. But on Friday morning, I did get a call from Pasadena, not from the Police department, but from a representative of an upstanding member of the community. Earl Bainbridge, a woman's voice on the phone told me, would like me to pay him a visit. She asked me to be there at noon, which meant there was a good chance I would arrive in that narrow window between when Earl was fully awake, but had not yet imbibed his first cocktail of the day.

Pasadena was no longer beset by the scorching heat of the past few weeks, although it was still plenty warm by the time I arrived at Earl's. But whether it be the height of summer or the dead of winter, the estate always looked the same; the pine trees were always full and the grass was always lush. No matter how many times I visited, I could not help but be taken in by the Tudor design and the colorful landscaping, all surrounded by that regal stone fence. Earl had remarkable taste, or more likely, someone in his lineage did. He might have been the bane of my existence the past few weeks, but having access to the Bainbridge Estate at least provided me with a glimpse into this privileged world. It was a world in which I couldn't afford to reside, might not even want to, but it was intoxicating just to be able to visit it occasionally. I pressed the button next to the intercom in front of the gate, but instead of being required to identify myself, the black gates simply opened, and I slowly drove inside the grounds, parking carefully on the cobblestone driveway.

A maid in a frilly black and white uniform led me inside, through a foyer featuring a spectacular crystal chandelier, then down a deeply carpeted hallway lined with dark wood. We wound up in a spacious breakfast nook, where Earl Bainbridge sat at a mahogany table, wearing a maroon robe over his pajamas. In front of him was a cup of black coffee and a plate containing what looked like two brown eggs inside thin silver egg cups. The servant took a device that looked like a cross between a pair of scissors and a cigar cutter, and used it to neatly slice the top sections of both eggs. The soft orange yolks oozed slightly out of their shells, and a couple of drops slid down the side. Earl motioned for me to sit down as he picked up a small, neatly cut, rectangular stick of toast and dipped it into one of the eggs. He didn't offer any to me and I didn't bother asking. It was very plain; Earl was the lord, I was merely the hired help.

"So Burnside," he began as he took a bite.

"Good morning, Earl. Or good afternoon, as the case may be."

"Yes, I suppose it technically is after noon. Thanks for coming by. I was hoping you'd call with an update on the case."

"Nothing to update right now. I've hit a dead end on the missing funds. No one's talking. I might have a chance at getting some help from the police, but not yet. I think it might be a long shot."

"Well," Earl said between bites, taking a lace napkin and wiping some errant yolk from his mouth. "I had a feeling you were going to come up empty. I've actually learned a few tidbits myself. Not about the money, I'm still holding you accountable there. But I've found out some interesting things about all that other unpleasantness that's been going on."

"By unpleasantness, you mean the murders," I said, feeling a need to clarify.

"Yes, yes, one of the boys down at the club has a grandson who works in the prosecutor's office. The Pasadena cops did some DNA testing. Preliminary results, mind you. The detectives said you were barking up the right tree after all."

"How so?

"Vicki Sailor," he said, picking up another stick of toast. "Student at the school, I guess. She was friendly with that history teacher, what's his name again?"

"Fowler. Jason Fowler."

"Yes, Fowler. So the cops picked her up this week. They've been trying to get her to confess. No murder weapon was found yet, but they've got something on her. I guess the detectives found her underwear and tested it. You know they found it in Fowler's office in the school? Guess she forgot it. Or maybe he wanted a souvenir. Trophy or something like that. Anyway, the DNA came back positive, those panties were hers. Preliminary, I'm told, but they think it's solid. Now they're trying to tie her to Bob Greenland. Be nice if they could wrap both of them murders up before the game tonight."

I shook my head. "A little too neat. And they'd still need to establish a motive."

"Oh, the cops'll figure something out. This town has a good police force. They'll yank it out of her."

"Lovely," I said.

Earl smiled an ugly smile. "It all fits together, doesn't it? Two people get stabbed within a week at that same damned school. They'll piece together a motive. The cops are convinced she's the one, anyway."

"Something doesn't add up here. Bob Greenland have any enemies you know of?"

"Besides me?" he cackled.

"Come on, Earl," I said, starting to get very weary of him.

"Oh, there was that guy Bob took apart, the parent of some player a few years back. Stan Weekes, I think, yeah, that's who the parent was. Back when Bob was coaching at the school. Weekes was mad that his kid was riding the bench, so he gave Bob a piece of his mind. Guess he said the wrong thing and really set Bob off. Stan wound up in the hospital. Cost Bob Greenland his career in the end."

"You know this Stan Weekes?"

"Nope, they weren't a Pasadena family. Oh, they might have lived here, but they didn't run in our circles. They weren't part of our crowd."

"Know where I might find him?" I asked.

"Heard he moved a while back. Arizona. Health problems. That's all I know. Why?"

"Just curious. Obviously someone did this. I'm just not sold on Vicki Sailor."

"Yeah, well, I have to tell you, this thing, these murders? It's really messing up the team. Just when Austin gets his big break, he gets to start at quarterback tonight, but now this nastiness with Bob Greenland happens. You know, Austin told me Dash used to have a thing with that Vicki. The girl's trying to pin the whole thing on Dash's mom. Can you believe that? Girl said she walked in on Skye screwing the teacher, but no one's paying much attention to that. The cops are convinced it's Vicki. Thanks to you. I guess you're the one who gave them the tip."

"Yeah," I muttered. "That's just swell."

"Ah, relax. You just focus on finding out about my money. Now what did you say about working with the police on figuring this out?"

"Look, Earl. I asked the detectives for a favor. Sometimes they deliver, sometimes they don't. I'll keep working it, but it may be a dry hole here. The truth will come out eventually. I'm just not sure when. And I don't know that it's a good use of my time or your money for me to keep plugging away at this."

"My money?" he looked at me. "I've paid you a lot of money already, Burnside. I expect results. Don't tell me you're going to pad the bill now. Extra days?"

I was reluctant to remind him that a lot of his payment included a past-due bill that was almost a decade in arrears. "No, Earl. I'm not planning to charge you extra right now. But I've been putting in some long days on this, a good bit more than the four days you paid for up front. Your retainer's spent. Maybe we'll get some details out of this, maybe we won't."

Earl gave me a long, hard glare. "I didn't like how your work ended last time. That's why I didn't pay you then. And I'm not liking how your work is going this time, either. You remember that."

I stared at him. "Earl."

"Yes?"

"Are you threatening me?"

"Now you look here, Burnside. I'm just saying that I'm a man who's used to getting what he wants. And I want to know what happened to all my money. I know I won't get it back. But I have a right to know what hole it went down."

*

Not having been invited to lunch at the Bainbridge Estate, I made my way back to Colorado Boulevard, parked, and walked around for a while. The St. Dismas football game wouldn't kick off for another six hours, so I had ample time to kill. I didn't think anything positive would emerge from yet another visit to the Pasadena police station, and anyone I wanted to speak with would most likely be at the game tonight.

Earl's poached egg breakfast probably got me in the mood, so I found a nice little bakery called Euro Pane which specialized in egg salad sandwiches. It was good egg salad. Actually, it was great egg salad, although one doesn't normally classify as "great" something that is so simple to prepare. It reminded me of how certain Chinese food critics will judge a restaurant on its orange chicken. While orange chicken is hardly a sophisticated dish, the thinking goes that if a chef can't be bothered to perform the basics properly, there is little point in assessing their more nuanced dishes.

With an abundance of free time today, I did some window shopping along Old Town Pasadena, wandered around Vroman's Bookstore, took a much-needed nap in the back seat of my Pathfinder, and then had a six dollar cup of Rwandan coffee at a trendy cafe called *Intelligentsia*. It was a good cup of coffee, but not a six dollar cup of coffee. I wasn't sure what a six dollar cup of coffee would be like, other than I was convinced I'd know it when I'd tasted it. The cafe was fairly empty, and I lingered at my table, scouring through Internet sites for details on Rwandan coffee. I found little. Maybe I was paying for the atmosphere, although paying six dollars to sit in a near-empty coffee house with the interior painted black and the ceiling strung with over a hundred chartreuse colored radio bulbs didn't strike me as a good deal for the money.

I arrived at St. Dismas Field two hours before kickoff. The school was playing Bishop Amat, and the visiting team was already on the grass, stretching and limbering up. There were a few people sprinkled around the bleachers. I saw one who looked quite familiar. The last time I saw her she was wearing a skimpy white bikini. Today she was only slightly more covered, wearing a blue halter and shorts. Skye Farsakian looked up at me as I approached, but did not say anything. She looked forlorn. Or maybe forsaken. I sat down next to her, and we both stared wordlessly out at the field for a while. Finally I spoke.

"I understand the police took your statement."

"Yes. Among other things. Thanks to you," she said in a detached way.

"Me?"

"You told the police about Vicki Sailor. And after they questioned her, Vicki Sailor had the gall to accuse me of murder. And the police wanted to run a DNA test on me."

"Sorry. But I heard the police are looking at her as the prime suspect."

"They should be," Skye said. "But to divert things, apparently Vicki gave the police my name. Told them I was having an affair with Jason. And of course, after people have affairs, they always murder them, don't they?"

I didn't bother informing Skye that I was the one who mentioned her Jason Fowler affair to the police, in exchange for the remote possibility of some information on what was, by comparison, the trite issue of some missing funds. Passing along scuttlebutt from an unreliable teenage source wasn't something I was proud of. But when a murder happens and the suspect is still at large, keeping confidences is not always a wise move. I turned to look at Skye. A few glistening tears were forming in her blue eyes. One tumbled out and rolled down her cheek.

"If you didn't do it, you shouldn't have anything to worry about," I said and instantly regretted it. The St. Dismas team was slowly making its way onto the field. I caught a glimpse of Dash Farsakian, suited up but walking slowly. Even if Skye had nothing to do with murdering Jason Fowler it was only a matter of time before others would learn of their affair. And though she was separated and had every right to be romantically involved with whomever she chose, she still had a son at the school. For a teenager, the loss of respect and the whispers about his mother's private affairs could be devastating.

"I liked Jason," she said, not looking at me. "It wasn't an intense relationship. But I liked him. And I liked the idea of being with a man again. This has been such a rough year for me. And it just keeps getting worse and worse."

By now she had started to openly weep. A few parents in the stands turned to look at us. None came over to find out what was going on or to comfort her. I wanted to put my arm around her, but that could have easily been taken the wrong way. Finally, she reached into her bag and took out a few tissues.

"I'm sorry," she said.

"Don't be. This is a very bad time. Understandable."

"I'm just afraid this nightmare is going to get worse."

"How so?" I asked.

"Whoever did this," she sobbed. "They're still out there. I'm petrified they'll strike again."

She made a good point. Whoever killed Jason Fowler and Bob Greenland had to have been furious with them. They wanted them to die in a very painful and personal way. Killing someone with a gun can be dispassionate and coldly efficient; it could also be done from a distance. But killing with a knife is an act of passion, the product of emotional rage and fury. Stabbing someone to death involves a closeness and an intimacy. To do so twice in one week bordered on the pathological.

I didn't have a response to this, but I did have another question. She might or might know the answer, but it was worth asking.

"Have you heard how Noah is?"

Skye wiped some tears away. "Managing. Coping, I guess. Losing your father this young and in this way? Horrible. I haven't spoken to Stacy, but I heard other parents have. Devastating for her, obviously. Losing her husband, and almost losing her son a few days earlier. I don't know how she could handle it."

People slowly began filing into the stands. I quietly said goodbye and moved up to the top of the bleachers. The crowd was subdued for the most part, parents acknowledging one another with a short wave and a few brief conversations. I also saw a few familiar faces, college scouts who nodded to me. One turned out to be a guy I had known for decades, Toa Latui, a gigantic offensive tackle who began playing for USC the year after I graduated. He weighed over 350 pounds when he came into college, and he might be even heavier now.

"I don't believe it," he said, his breathing a little unsteady after climbing all the way up the bleachers. "Man, if it isn't Burnside. What's the matter? Don't like sitting at field level?"

"Toa, you're looking fit as always," I chuckled.

"Ha! The kids keep me young."

"What are you doing these days?"

"Coaching the O-line down at San Diego State. Good gig, this is my second year. I was up in Utah for a long time, but, hey, you know. This place is almost home."

"Almost," I said. "How come you're not coaching where you grew up in Hawaii?"

"I'd love to," he said. "But everyone wants to coach there. Then they go into semi-retirement. Rainbows haven't had a good team in years."

"Who are you looking at here?" I asked.

"Ah, got my eye on a few linemen. Couple of guys on Bishop Amat. Would've loved to get that Greenland kid, but he'd have been a long shot for us. Plus, with everything that's gone on, that kid's a huge question mark right now. But this Farsakian guy here might be a good fit for us."

I smiled and pointed about eight rows down. "There's his mom. Name's Skye Farsakian."

Toa looked down and licked his lips. "Nice. Kid just took a step up toward getting an offer."

"I can introduce you if you like."

"Nah. I'm not shy. But thanks for the tip."

"Anyone else you're looking at here?"

"Mostly from Bishop Amat. I wish Greenland was playing tonight. Kind of tough to evaluate the team without him. Everything changes when the starting quarterback's out."

I nodded. We made a little more small talk and Toa went off. I noticed the two blonde girls I met the week before, Ivy and Jasmine, seated themselves about twenty feet away from me. I tried to talk to a few parents, but most didn't want to be bothered. I didn't even make an attempt at approaching the two girls. I got the feeling people were beginning to wonder why I kept coming around here. I was starting to wonder the same thing.

The game began and it quickly turned into a lopsided affair. St. Dismas got the ball first, and the newly appointed quarterback, Austin Bainbridge, went back to pass on the first play. Within seconds, the blocking collapsed and Austin was buried under a sea of white jerseys. An audible groan was heard from the crowd. I noticed Dash Farsakian limping badly and needed to come out of the game. The next play was more of the same, and by the end of the first half, St. Dismas was behind 28-7, with Austin completing only a couple of passes. Their lone touchdown came when Austin was forced to scramble and raced up the sideline, showing surprising speed. The game eventually became a rout, with Bishop Amat winning 55-14.

The St. Dismas fans filed out dejectedly. I saw Duke Savich lecturing the team on the sidelines, but the players all had their heads down and I doubt they were listening to him. They shuffled their feet and a few looked away. As I walked past the team, Curly Underwood noticed me and motioned for me to come over.

"Tough game," I said.

"Not going to get much better for a while."

"Is Noah coming back?"

"Maybe. I spoke with him yesterday. Says he's feeling good, but we'll need a doctor's okay. And the mom needs to okay it, too."

"That might be harder."

"Might be," he said. "So how come you still coming around these parts?"

I shrugged. "Well, like I said from the beginning, a certain someone wants to know what happened to his donation."

Curly Underwood shook his head. "Look, I can't tell you much," he sighed. "But if it will make you stop coming around here, I can assure you the money wound up going to a good cause."

"What do you mean?"

"Just what I said."

"That's not a lot to go on," I said.

"It's all I can tell you," he responded. "And I may have even said too much as it is."

I gave him a long stare. He stared back. Finally, we both went our separate ways.

## *Thirteen*

The next morning, Gail and I took the opportunity to treat Marcus to pancakes at IHOP. He especially loved the ones where they painted a smiley face on the top pancake, using whipped cream and chocolate chips. One time I had made the mistake of bringing him to John O'Groats, a more sophisticated restaurant. In addition to listening to him complain that blueberries had no place inside of pancakes, he asked why there weren't any kids like him eating there. I tried to tell him this was more of a grownups' place, but with the plethora of entertainment executives at nearby tables, I wasn't fully convinced this was true. I finally recognized that while Marcus occasionally liked to feel special by going to some of our restaurants, what really made him happy was going to places that were more welcoming to people like him. And that meant places that had the wisdom to put chocolate chips on their pancakes.

We got home and played a few board games with Marcus, but by mid-afternoon, I grew a little antsy and went off to sit at my desk and brood. I had yet to solve the puzzle that Earl Bainbridge had paid me to solve. The

Pasadena detectives hadn't delivered the paperwork I had politely requested. And despite Curly Underwood's insinuation that Earl's money had been well-spent on a worthy and noble cause, I still harbored doubts. The two cases might not be linked at all, but I continued to cling to the fading hope that if I solved one of them, the other would somehow fall magically into place. After a while, Chewy walked in with a stuffed toy dinosaur in her mouth, and pushed it against my hand. We played tug-of-war for a while, and I remembered to let her win most of the time. Then she pressed her cold nose against my hand for a long second, her signal that it was time to eat. I glanced at my watch and was surprised to see it was after 5:00 p.m. The afternoon had somehow disappeared. I gave Chewy a bowl of kibble, and Gail and I made plans for dinner.

It was still warm out, and warm weather in Los Angeles meant it was barbecue season. It didn't matter if it was mid-September or mid-February, the siren call of the grill was always near. Gail went over to Costco and picked up three thick rib-eye steaks, sensing I would probably be called upon to help Marcus finish his. I grilled them over charcoal, as was my preference. If you're going to be old-school, you need to be old-school all the way. The hickory marinade which Gail had soaked them in dripped down onto the coals, and the occasional orange flame sparked upward over the meat. After flipping them a few times and getting a nice char on their surface, I estimated that they were medium-rare. Gail assured me that she wasn't questioning my culinary judgment when she sliced one open and inspected the color. She merely wanted to ensure Marcus would be able to eat these comfortably. This, of course, was code for not wanting to be up with Marcus in the middle of the night, in case his process of peristalsis didn't move through the appropriate stages.

As I started cutting into Marcus's steak, I began to come upon some obstacles. The knife was far from razor sharp, an especially knotty problem since I needed to cut the pieces very small. A three year old does not have a large mouth or throat. So whereas it would not have been a big issue for me to bite off more than I could chew, this was not a burden I could put on a young child. Providing Marcus with what he could handle was always a pre-eminent concern. I struggled with the knife, but was finally able to cut his well-marbled rib-eye into tiny, bite-size pieces that he could manage. As was his routine, he picked a piece up with his fingers, chewed it for an inordinate time before swallowing, made a gesture of approval, and then reached for another one.

"These knives seem a bit dull," I commented as I continued to work on cutting some more miniscule pieces.

"They were a wedding present," Gail said as she began cutting into her steak. "The Fishers gave these to us."

"I suppose they could use some sharpening," I said. "It's been four years since we got married."

"Time flies," she said as she took a bite and smiled appreciatively. "This is wonderful. You did a great job. The master griller."

I smiled and swiped a few more tiny pieces onto Marcus's plate. He happily picked another one up, continuing to chew slowly and thoughtfully.

"You like?" I asked.

"Uh-huh," he replied, savoring the morsel. "This is great."

I cut a piece of mine, albeit with continued difficulty, and tasted it. Nice. Tender, smoky, flavorful. Looking down at my knife, I began to examine it. I stopped eating and took a closer look. The blade wasn't that old, but it certainly wasn't very sharp. I thought about which steak knives might be sharper. I leaned back in my chair and held the knife up to the light.

"What are you doing, Daddy?" Marcus asked.

"Yes, sweetie," Gail chimed in. "Just what are you doing?"

I looked at them and smiled. "Detective work."

"You can do that at the dinner table?" Marcus asked, eyes wide.

"I think I can."

"I want a job like that!" he said.

I smiled at Marcus. Gail looked a little apprehensive. "You can have any job you set your mind to," she told him.

"Daddy?"

"Yes, Marcus?" I said, putting the knife back down and smiling broadly.

"Have you finished your detec ... what did you say?"

"Detective work," I said. "And yes. I think so. I think I may have just solved the case."

"Really?" he asked. " Just by eating steak? Just like that? "

"Yes," I smiled. "Just like that."

\*

As difficult as it was to cut, I certainly enjoyed my steak. And I was finally starting to enjoy my weekend as well. While I briefly considered driving back to Pasadena that night, I knew the thing I was after would still be there the next day. So Saturday night was spent playing more games and watching a movie with Gail and Marcus. I did slip away for a minute to call Al Diamond and confirm he would be punching the clock on a Sunday afternoon. I suggested he might want to come in by lunchtime. He suggested I better have something darned good for him.

The Valley Steakhouse in Pasadena had been around for many decades, and was famous for something called a culotte steak. This was a top sirloin cut, a piece of meat that more closely resembled a softball then what one would normally think of when ordering a restaurant steak. The online menu proudly pointed out that there were only two culotte steaks on the steer, and while this might suggest a rare delicacy, I also considered that there were only two ears on the animal as well, and I certainly had no intention of eating those.

The restaurant opened before noon, but when I arrived at 12:30 p.m., there was only one other table occupied. The interior was warm, maybe the air conditioning had not been turned on yet, maybe they were trying to save money on utilities. I wore a sports jacket, and while a little uncomfortable, I kept it on the whole time. In addition to covering my holstered pistol, I'd need the jacket for more practical purposes.

This was an older-style steakhouse, the walls were layered with the kind of plastic wood paneling that fooled no one and only contributed to the cheap feel of the dining room. This was nothing like Morton's or Ruth's Chris, but to its credit, it didn't bill itself as a premium steakhouse. This restaurant struck me as part of a dying breed, joints that served up cheap drinks and cheap steaks at a good value, but paled in comparison to newer establishments. This was certainly old-school, and while that would normally be a point in its favor from my perspective, old-school was not always so terrific.

The bored hostess seated me, took my drink order for an iced tea, and returned with it about fifteen minutes later. Grudgingly, she wrote down my lunch order at the same time. I had no idea if there were any waiters working there. Clearly, business was not good, and no one looked happy.

"Kind of slow today," I said.

"Kind of slow every day," she replied.

"That why the staff is so lean?"

She shook her head. "The owner cut our wages a few times. We also think he's dipping into the tip pool. So people keep leaving."

I nodded warily and wondered if having someone taste my food might be an idea, although I couldn't imagine who would be interested in that line of work. My culotte steak arrived a little while later, cooked well-done instead of medium-rare, and tasting decidedly ordinary. But the knife they brought me worked remarkably well. It had a serrated edge, and I decided that rather than try and sharpen ours at home, maybe getting a replacement set was a better idea. I ate about half of the culotte steak before concluding my rib-eye last night was far superior. Then I then turned my attention to the real reason for entering this dingy place.

The absence of a crowd made my task a little trickier. In a hectic, bustling restaurant, no one bothers to watch you closely; there are too many other things going on. In an empty restaurant, however, you never know who's observing your moves. I looked around and saw a tired bartender wiping down a counter, and a few busboys whispering in a corner. The owner of the restaurant, his large body somewhat camouflaged by a suit and tie, had waddled into the main room for a minute. His eyes darted about the room, scanned me briefly, but seemingly without any recognition, and then turned around to talk with the hostess. I reached over, placed the knife inside of my napkin, wiped it down, and wrapped it tightly. I then surreptitiously slipped it into the breast pocket of my jacket, pointed downward, right next to my .357. While this was unlikely to be the actual knife that killed either Jason Fowler or Bob Greenland, it was an important one to examine.

I got the attention of the hostess across the room and used my fingers to make a squiggly motion to signify I'd like the check. A few minutes later, she walked up and presented it to me. I paid in cash, not wanting to leave a calling card that I had been there, but also not wanting to wait the additional fifteen minutes it would undoubtedly take to run my credit card. I strode purposefully out the door and toward my Pathfinder.

"Hey!" a voice suddenly called out behind me. "Hey, you!"

I turned and saw the oversized body of Wally Farsakian coming toward me. From a distance, he simply looked big, not fat. But as he drew closer, I saw that the light gray suit had been carefully tailored to hide his massive gut. He moved quickly for a big man. His face was grim and a couple of bandages were evident on his right hand.

"Wait up, you!"

"I'm waiting," I said.

"You're that detective guy, right?"

"Right," I answered, not sure that I liked that reference any better than being called 'that USC guy.'

"What are you doing here?"

"Eating lunch. Or what passes for it."

"My hostess said you took something. What'd you take?"

"Probably a dose of indigestion."

His mouth curled. "You have a big mouth."

"I know. I get a lot of complaints about it."

"My business isn't doing well, in case you hadn't noticed," he snarled.

"I did notice. Maybe there's a reason. The only thing worse than the food here is the service."

A scowl formed on his face and his breathing started to escalate, sure signs that the conversation was about to escalate from words into something else very quickly. He flung his arms forward in a way that fighters do to loosen up. It wasn't so much of a tell, as a warning. This was a big man who was used to intimidating people. The problem he was about to encounter was that I didn't get intimidated easily.

"What did you take from my restaurant?" he repeated. "I can't have people stealing from me."

"Sure. That would be illegal."

"Give me that knife," he ordered.

"No."

He stared at me, then took a couple of steps back, removed his coat and began to loosen his tie. I knew what was coming, and I knew that fighting a man who outweighed you by a hundred pounds was not an event to be welcomed. What I could make up in the speed of throwing punches, and in the quickness of darting to and fro, could easily be offset by his landing just one solid punch. There were reasons fighters had weight classes. A good big man could take a good little man most of the time. I wasn't so little, but as Einstein postulated, it's all relative. I took two quick steps forward, grabbed him by the front of his starched white shirt, pulled him slightly toward me and drove my knee squarely up into his groin.

Wally Farsakian dropped to the ground and doubled over, his mouth agape. He began moaning slightly. Fortunately, this being a Sunday afternoon, the street had no foot traffic. But a couple of Latino busboys emerged from the restaurant and started to approach. I pointed a finger at them and told them to stop where they were. They didn't stop, possibly because they didn't care what I said, or possibly because they didn't speak English. I drew my .357 and repeated my directive to halt. This time they stopped cold. Brandishing a pistol has become the universal sign to not move.

"I'm ... going to have you ... arrested," managed Wally Farsakian, his uneven voice spewing out words in a staccato manner.

"Are you now?" I asked. "On what charge? Assaulting you before you assaulted me?"

"You're a wise guy ... and you're going to get yours."

"No, I'm not," I said, watching him carefully. "The opposite's going to happen. You're going to jail for murder. Maybe two murders."

"Says who? You can't ... prove shit," he panted. "Those knives I used ... they're long gone. Buried in the trash. No murder weapons. No charges filed. I know ... how this works."

"So you figured you'd kill two men just because they were screwing your ex? You couldn't just move on with your life?"

"We're still married," he glared. "Skye and I were getting back together. Those two assholes were ... they were messing things up. They had it coming to them. Fowler and Greenland. Pair of slimy bastards."

"No one has murder coming to them. Not for any reason. And certainly not because they had an affair."

"They were doing it in public!" he barked, starting to get his bearings back. "All over the place! In an office, behind the bleachers. They were humiliating my wife!"

"Her choice, wasn't it?"

Farsakian glared angrily. "Yeah. And I chose to carve them up for it. Life is full of choices, ain't it? And you can't prove shit."

Life was indeed full of choices, and at that point, it was my choice to pull out my phone with my left hand and punch Al Diamond's number. I told him he had a choice to get down here on the double and solve two murders. He asked what was going on and I repeated he needed to get down to the Valley Steakhouse immediately, before another person got killed. Farsakian started to stand up. I suggested to Diamond that he bring uniformed backup and tell them to use the sirens. The detective tried to question me further, but this wasn't the time for an in-depth discussion. I hung up, pointed my gun at Farsakian, and ordered him to stay where he was.

I glanced over at the two busboys. They were staring at us in awe. This wasn't going to be their typical day at work, or typical of any of their work days. I wondered if they truly grasped what was going on, and why a patron who had just finished his sub-par meal was detaining their boss at gunpoint. It couldn't have only been about the food. I might have been able to dredge up enough high school Spanish to make myself understood, although maintaining any sort of dialogue was a different story. But at that moment, things started to crystallize. Wally Farsakian became more aware of his surroundings, that it was not merely the two of us alone on the sidewalk, with him revealing a secret which might have irreparable consequences. It was no longer his word against mine. He noticed the busboys, and a sick look crossed his face.

"*Felipe. Pedro. Abandonas*," he said.

"No, boss," one of them replied. "We're not leaving."

"You both speak English?" I queried.

They both nodded.

"And you understood everything your boss just said?"

They nodded again.

I stared at them and began to feel better about things. They apparently took my stare as some sort of disrespect, an indication of disbelief that they actually understood and comprehended the magnitude of what Wally Farsakian had just uttered.

"Look," the first one declared in English that was at least as good as mine. "We were born in fucking East L.A. Of course we speak English. We know exactly what that cheap prick was saying. He stabbed two people to death."

## *Fourteen*

The mere mention of a need for backup apparently spurred Al Diamond into full-throttled action mode. A pair of black and white squad cars, sirens blaring, roared up less than one minute later, with Detective Diamond arriving shortly thereafter in an unmarked vehicle. I holstered my weapon as they spun around the corner, thus negating any need for the uniforms to force me to spread eagle against the wall, as they did Wally Farsakian when he belligerently demanded my arrest. Diamond himself slapped the cuffs on him, and, after a brief consultation, provided me and the two busboys with a free ride over to the police station for questioning.

I gave my statement to Diamond at his desk in the squad room. He mostly listened, asking an occasional probing question here and there. The knife I had procured from the Valley Steakhouse was quickly shepherded over to Forensics; it wouldn't take long to determine if this was the same model knife that killed Jason Fowler and Bob Greenland. And with three witnesses swearing they heard a confession, along with a rock solid motive, Wally Farsakian had apparently broken down and succumbed to the myriad of circumstantial evidence and confessed. A more street-savvy criminal might have clammed up, demanded an attorney and insisted law enforcement build what might be a tenuous case. But when someone who's never committed a serious crime is told they are facing a near-certain death penalty unless they came clean, they often become inclined to talk. Sometimes they are too emotionally exhausted to keep up the lie; a guilty conscience can place an inordinate amount of strain on a person's psyche.

"Where's Turco?" I asked as we were finishing up. "Gone fishing again?"

"Nah," Diamond said and put his feet up on the table. "His weekend with the kids. Divorced. You know."

I didn't know, and hoped I'd never know the details of what came along with that life. When I was on the job, I saw it second hand, and from my vantage point it was rarely enviable. The long hours and intense work often meant high burn-out rates, with officers bringing home their on-the-job problems, and spouses not reacting well to the added burden. Law enforcement had an above-average divorce rate. A lot of L.A. cops were divorced and didn't see their kids much. And when they did, they were usually too tired to do a lot with them.

"So tell me something, Detective," I said, wondering how much he'd be willing to share. "Who else were you looking at for this?"

Diamond paused for a moment. "We started with the coach, that Savich guy. Your tip about that knife in his office was reasonable, it just didn't pan out. We looked at a lot of people. The one we had the most interest in was the kid. The one with the weird name."

"Dashiell?" I asked. "Dash Farsakian?"

"Yeah. Kid had been dating that Vicki Sailor, the girl who said she walked in on Fowler and Mrs. Farsakian. Figured Vicki told her boyfriend about it, so we pressed him. Kid insisted he knew nothing about any of this. Looks like he was telling the truth all along. Not a bad kid, just had a slut for a mother and a lying murderer for a father. His bad luck, I guess."

"Again, you sure have a knack for describing things."

"Hey, I don't get paid to be a nice guy."

"Obviously," I noted.

"Yeah, and that knife in Savich's office was another good tip of yours that didn't pan out and wasted our time. I know. You meant well."

I took a deep breath and let it out. "Look, Detective, everything is related here. Sure, that knife I found was too dull to cut anything more than mud out of a bunch of cleats. But because it was dull, it led me to find out the murder weapon was serrated. And where better place to find a serrated knife than a steakhouse?"

"Got it. Point taken."

"And by the way, I also knew Vicki had been going out with Dash. But I spoke with the kid right before Greenland's body was found, and it was found right behind where we were seated in the bleachers. If Dash was the culprit, he'd have had to be a complete sociopath to sit there calmly after he killed someone. He didn't fit the type. So I ruled him out."

"Okay," he said, holding up his hands. "You don't have to get sore about it."

"Sure," I said and continued on. "But what about the girl's underwear that was found in Fowler's office? My understanding is they belonged to Vicki Sailor."

Diamond gave me a funny look. "You heard about that?"

"I hear about a lot of things. Then I try and piece them all together. Sometimes the puzzle makes sense. It's what I do."

"Yeah. Okay. We did find underwear and we did link it back to the girl, Vicki. But Dash admitted he took a pair from her bedroom. Kind of as a joke, hey, he's a teenager. Apparently Skye found it while cleaning his room, and Dash told her whose it was. Skye mentions it to Wally, Wally takes it from Dash's room. He thought Vicki was doing the teacher. I guess Wally thought if he planted it in Fowler's office, we might link the murder back to Vicki Sailor. Puts a wall between Wally and the crime. Or so he thought anyway."

I shook my head. "What a genius," I said dryly.

"Yeah. Girl had no motive, and she certainly didn't look like she could knife two grown men. Again, you talk with some of these people, and you can't see how they could commit one murder, much less two. That was part of why this whole case was so baffling. If a gun were used, maybe. But a knife? That's different."

"Of course," I said. "So tell me. Did Wally Farsakian ever register as a suspect with you guys?"

"Um, yeah. You think?" he said. "Look, we finally got the DNA back on Greenland a few days ago. The lab took a while. Greenland had been with Skye right before the attack. We had talked to both Skye and Wally, but at the time, we had nothing tangible on either. And I couldn't believe that a woman would stab both guys."

"What happened when you spoke with Wally Farsakian?"

"Was calm, had an alibi for the time of both murders. Said he was at his restaurant, in the back office the whole time. A couple of employees backed up his story. I guess they were reluctant to go against their boss. So we had nothing firm on him. Couldn't detain him."

"Nobody thought that the owner of a steakhouse might have had access to some sharp knives?"

"Come on, Burnside. Unlike you, we don't have the right to go seize private property without a warrant. And he's hardly the only person in Pasadena that owns kitchen knives."

"The fact that you didn't even check it out notwithstanding."

"Hey, smart guy, ease up on the snarky remarks. You know, we could charge you with petty theft for taking that knife today."

I stared at him. "Really? Go ahead. I'm sure the *Star-News* would love to run a series of articles on how the incompetent Pasadena police arrested the P.I. who cracked a double murder case that they couldn't. How would you like that headline to read?"

"All right, all right."

"And I suppose you could also charge me with assaulting a murderer. Or the fact that the item I stole -- allegedly -- was taken solely to give to your forensics lab. And had I not taken it, our friend Wally Farsakian wouldn't have confronted me. And he wouldn't have confessed to those murders in front of three witnesses. I didn't plan on that happening. But did I not make your job a whole lot easier today?"

Diamond gave an audible groan. "I said all right, damn it. Cripes. You don't know when to quit. You have a real attitude problem, you know that?"

"Yes. Or so I've been told. So back to the knife. You had to have known that the one that killed Fowler was serrated."

"Yeah. And the blade was fishtailed at the end. Like I said, Forensics just came back with that. We don't have LAPD resources. We make do with what we have."

"No one thought to check Farsakian's hands for cuts? You stab someone hard enough to kill them, the force of it usually causes nicks in the palm or fingers. His hands had bandages on them. You might say he had blood on his hands."

"Are you going to keep busting our balls over this? No, we didn't think to check. Pasadena doesn't get a lot of knifings. It's not like L.A. It's a safe place to live. Some of this is new to us. Most of what we work on here are burglaries, car break-ins, neighbor disputes. That kind of thing."

"Okay," I sighed. "Understood. I just didn't like that crack about you charging me with theft."

"Look, we thank you for your help. I know that sort of thing sometimes goes unsaid, but we do appreciate your staying on this case. I don't quite know why you did, but we're grateful for it."

"You're welcome," I said. "Which brings me to one last matter."

Diamond looked at me. "What now?"

"I had asked you about some large checks St. Dismas was writing on an account from Crown Bank. Charity or something. Anything come of that?"

A small smile, or perhaps more of a smirk crossed Diamond's face. "If I recall," he said, "you were giving us tips that were going to pan out on the murder cases. Turns out those tips were wrong."

I rolled my eyes. "Sure they were. And I also delivered a murderer to you. You got the collar and none of your uniforms were in the slightest danger. When you cracked the case, Wally was down on his knees holding his crotch. Thanks to me. But yes, those tips I gave you did not lead directly to Wally Farsakian. Sorry. My bad."

Diamond's expression did not change as he reached into a drawer and pulled out a large, yellowish envelope and handed it to me.

"Here you go. It's got what you want in there."

"Why thank you, Detective," I said. "That's most kind of you."

"You do good work, Burnside. You're a bit of a jerk at times, and you have a big mouth. But you do good work."

I smiled back at him and briefly reveled in the moment. "Aw, Detective," I said. "You're going to make me blush."

*

I called my soon-to-be erstwhile client and asked for an appointment on Monday, giving me a little time to pore over the bank statements. Earl Bainbridge responded by suggesting 5:00 p.m. A late-afternoon meeting meant entering and exiting Pasadena in rush hour, an idea I didn't relish. But I also recognized I wouldn't be coming up this way much anymore. And the 5:00 p.m. time meant something important to Earl, as he could not only get in 18 holes of golf, but he could also squeeze me in before the kickoff of Monday Night Football. Apparently, the Rams were playing.

It was pleasant and warm when I arrived at the Bainbridge Estate at two minutes before 5:00. I pulled onto the cobblestone driveway, climbed out of my Pathfinder and took a long, admiring look at the Tudor-style mansion. There were many beautiful homes in L.A., but this would always be one of my favorites. I only wished it belonged to someone else.

The maid led me into a parlor area with soft, pastel paintings on the wall and plush, maroon carpeting covering the floor. There were two red-striped sofas facing each other, with a glass coffee table in between, held up by four slabs of red oak. An empty stone fireplace was situated off in a corner. A white baby grand piano sat nearby, but it had the clean, polished look of a work of art, something to behold, rather than an instrument on which to play music.

"Burnside," came a voice from the doorway. "Right on time. Thanks for being prompt."

"Not a problem, Earl. I don't want to keep you from the Rams game. You're aware they've invented DVRs, aren't you?"

"Always with the wisecracks," he said and sat down on one of the red-striped sofas. He motioned for me to sit on the other. "What do you have for me?"

I sat down across from him. The couch certainly looked gorgeous, it was undoubtedly very expensive and the material felt silky smooth. But surprisingly, it was not especially comfortable. I tossed the file on the coffee table. "There's your answer."

He looked at me and made no attempt at picking up the folder. "Give me the short version."

"All right," I said. I suppose when you have Earl's kind of money, you can pay others to do your reading for you. "It's the last two quarterly bank statements for the St. Dismas Charity Sports Foundation. There were two large checks written, one for thirty-five thousand, the other for forty thousand. They were both made out to Bob Greenland."

Earl slapped his knee and shook his head up and down vociferously. "I knew it. I knew it," he exclaimed. "Savich paid them to send Noah to the school. Was I right about that family?"

"Earl."

"Yeah?"

"Noah Greenland lost his father last week. Murdered. Are you going to crow about that, too?"

Earl sank back into the couch and stared off into space for a while. "I see your point," he finally said.

"Good."

"But it does paint a picture of corruption."

"I suppose it very well could. But what are you going to do about it? Again, Noah just lost his dad. The kid attempted suicide. His mother's practice isn't doing well. His football career is in limbo. Noah's a broken kid. Are you going to demand the family give you the money back? I spoke with Noah's mother a few weeks ago, I don't think Bob even told even her he was getting these checks."

Earl looked at me oddly, almost angrily, and I couldn't discern if he was considering my argument or getting ready to order me out of his house just prior to releasing the hounds.

"I don't like being deceived. And I don't like my money being redirected. Savich told me the money was going toward a new field, new uniforms, heck, even a Jumbotron was on the table. I don't like being lied to."

"You should have a word with Savich," I said, adding, "but don't tell him how you got hold of those documents. I had to pull some strings."

"Yes," he said. "I suppose you had to. And I have a few ideas about how to deal with Savich, don't you worry."

"Which are?" I asked. "You mentioned something about a board of directors."

"I did. But I also have some friends in the media. I'll handle this from here. Look, you did some good work for me, Burnside. You got me what I wanted."

"Thanks. But keep my name out of the press. I work for money now, not glory."

"Oh? Are you going to hit me up for more dough?"

"I did put in more than four days," I told him. "And I also needed to crack a couple of murder cases, in part, because my investigation got intertwined with the killings. The police had me in their sights as a person of interest."

"All right. Fine. Look. Send me a bill. You did what I asked you to do, even though you took your sweet time about it. I know you've been putting in the hours. I've heard you'd been poking around in lots of nooks and crannies around town. And I saw the article today in the *Star-News*. Wally Farsakian, I'll be darned. The paper didn't list you by name, but the police did mention he was detained by a private investigator. I'm sure that was you."

"It was," I said. "The police like to take credit for these things. Builds public confidence. At this point in my career, I'll settle for some extra money. Yes, I'll send you a bill. I'd appreciate it if you paid this one. Last time it took eight years. And I didn't even charge you interest."

Earl Bainbridge gave a snort, which might have been the closest thing I'd see to a laugh from him. In the background, I heard a door slam, and something heavy dropped on the floor.

"What's that?" I asked.

"Probably my kid," Earl said, "but he usually comes home later. Hey Austin! Come on in here!"

A few seconds later, Austin Bainbridge sauntered into the room. "Hey," he said.

"Coaches end practice early?" Earl asked.

"Nah. Had to cancel. The field was totally flooded."

"Ah, crap. The sprinklers again? How does this stuff keep happening?"

"The school finally figured it out," he said. "They brought out the DWP a bunch of times, had plumbers come in, they all said everything should be working fine. But it wasn't. So the school installed security cameras near the valves. Turns out someone was sneaking in and messing with the timer, setting the sprinklers off for hours on end."

"Who was it," Earl asked eagerly. "Someone from St. John Hershey? Never liked that school, they were always jealous of us. Plus, we have a game with them in a couple weeks."

"No, believe it or not, it was some teacher," Austin replied.

"Let me guess," I said. "Mary Swain."

"Yeah. How'd you know?" he asked, eyes wide.

"It's what I do," I smiled.

"Well, you're right," Austin said. "The school found out Ms. Swain had been the one doing this all along, and that's why she got fired. Guess she was really ticked off about it, and thought she could keep doing it. She wore a disguise, but her fingerprints were all over the valves. They finally got solid proof. We heard she's been arrested. Funny thing."

"What's that?"

"The timing was pretty good, today. Nobody on the team wanted to practice after we got wrecked so bad on

Friday night. Couldn't hurt to have a day off. Especially after we learned what happened to Dash's father."

"What do the guys on the team think about all that?" I asked.

"We feel bad for Dash, naturally," he said. "I've known him since forever. His dad, too. Wally's not a bad guy, just has a temper problem. Nobody thought it would ever come to this. But Dash's mom is in bad shape. Really busted up over this. Feels it's all her fault."

I nodded. Unintended as it might have been, had Skye not been sexually involved with multiple men, and doing it in such a precarious way, her husband wouldn't have committed these atrocious acts. Had Skye been more discreet, he might not have even known about her activities. But I suspected it was all very intentional.

"I imagine she feels a ton of guilt," I said.

"Yeah. Dash was telling me that Wally didn't want a divorce anymore. I guess she didn't want to take him back, but he wouldn't listen. So she had to give him a reason. Show him their marriage was over. That's why she did it with Mr. Fowler on his desk. And with Noah's dad on the grass behind the bleachers. She knew he would learn about it. Skye was egging him on. Just wanted Wally out of her life. Didn't think it would lead to all this."

I raised my eyebrows. "Skye told this to Dash?"

"Yeah, like I said, she feels horrible. I guess the night before Mr. Fowler got killed, Skye was up in his office. That's when Wally found out. Funny thing that Mr. Fowler was still there that late. I guess Wally waited until the next morning to kill him. Wanted to be alone with him."

I sighed. "Sounds like you've heard quite a story."

"More than I wanted to know. At this point, I just want to finish and go off to college. Leave this mess behind me. I can't get out of that school fast enough."

I looked at Earl, who was staring at his son, mouth open but bereft of any words. I didn't know if he had put it all together yet, but maybe he had. If I hadn't gone looking for Mary Swain that first evening when I visited St. Dismas, Fowler might have left work before Skye went up to his office. Maybe Wally would have never learned about their carnal embrace. Maybe if Earl had decided not to pay me, I wouldn't have even been in Pasadena that evening. Maybe if the Fishers had given us a better wedding present, I wouldn't have snapped the pieces together on Saturday night. And Wally Farsakian might never have been caught. I sighed and got up to leave. And made a mental note to go buy new steak knives this week. The serrated kind.

# *Fifteen*

I did make one final trek out to Pasadena, the purpose of which was not to collect more money from Earl Bainbridge. I had sent him an invoice and remarkably received payment a few days later, although it came without a thank you note. After allowing a few weeks to go by, and reading that St. Dismas had lost their fourth game in a row, I read a blurb on an internet recruiting site saying Noah Greenland would be returning to play quarterback for the Warriors. They were hosting St. John Hershey on Friday, and St. Dismas would also be playing in its first game under their new head coach.

There is something oddly connective about being a sports fan. You start watching a team a few times, even a team at the high school level, and a spark of interest emerges. It forms a bond. You're curious how certain players will perform and how the team will respond, particularly after they've been dealt adversity. Having watched a few of their games, and having both played and coached organized football, I was now very curious about this team. And harboring a strong interest in human nature, I was especially curious about Noah Greenland.

As was my recent custom, I got to the St. Dismas field early, sat high in the bleachers again, and watched the crowd filter in. The usual parents, friends, and college scouts. I gave a wave to the ones I knew, a few of them even waved back. But one person saw me and climbed up to the top row.

"Burnside," he said, shaking my hand.

"Chuck Mantle. Always a pleasure. Surprised to see you back here."

"We had a Thursday night game against Texas Tech. Home game. Freed me up to travel today. Figured I might take another crack at Noah. I spoke with him this week, and he sounded open to leaving California now."

I agreed. "A change of scenery might be a good idea for him. Just don't tell him there's a Pasadena in Texas, too."

"It's very different," he said.

"I would hope so."

"So. I've been hearing a lot about you, Burnside. That whole investigation thing. Sounds you played a big role."

"True."

"And you managed to take down a head coach. That's quite a scalp."

"I didn't take anyone down. Savich did it to himself. When you siphon money to a student's family, you're taking a risk. You better pray it doesn't become public," I said, recalling the *Star-Ledger's* exposé a few weeks ago. I guess one of Earl's cronies at the club had some juice in being able to catapult that into a front-page news story.

"I know. This sort of thing happens," Mantle said. "Much more in college than high school, but the world's changing. High school isn't the same as when we were there. And Savich broke the cardinal rule."

"What's that?"

"Don't get caught."

"I guess there are some things that never change," I said. "Tell me something. Are you looking at any other St. Dismas kids besides Noah?"

"We're still looking at that Farsakian kid. Bit of a stretch, but I think San Diego State's more interested in him. With all that's been happening with his family, I guess he wants to stay near his mom. Each kid's different. Some want to get as far away from this place as possible. Others not so much. We're interested in Will Kingston. And we're also looking at that Bainbridge kid."

"Austin? You told me you didn't think he had the athleticism."

"Still not sure. He's got better speed than we thought, maybe we can convince him to give up on playing quarterback. I heard he didn't perform so well there the last few weeks. A walk-on as a receiver isn't beyond the realm for him if he's flexible on positions. He might even develop into a decent special teams player."

"You know that his dad's loaded."

"Yeah," he said. "Would save us a scholarship. That's one benefit of having a rich dad."

This was true, and not entirely fair. A kid from a wealthy family simply has more options. Doesn't guarantee success or even happiness, it only offers more choices. I started to ponder the idea of what was fair and what was not, and that anyone touched by the bloody spate of violence emanating from St. Dismas recently would have trouble believing that life was fair. I started to feel another headache coming on and tried to think of something else. Unfortunately, things began to get worse.

Chuck Mantle called out to a couple that was making its way up the bleachers toward us. They greeted Mantle in a warm way and pointedly ignored me. They asked about their son's chances of getting an offer from Mantle's school and complimented him on his team's win last night. I listened quietly for a few minutes, then interrupted them by saying hello. They gave me a cool look, and Chuck Mantle hastily said goodbye and climbed back down the bleachers.

"We certainly weren't expecting to see you here," Talley Kingston said, the icicles practically dripping on her every word.

"Couldn't stay away. I'm curious about Noah."

"Curious?" Buzz Kingston snapped. "Good for you. Frankly, we're pretty sick of this whole mess."

"I can imagine."

"Can you?" he demanded. "Can you imagine getting hauled in by the police and questioned about a murder? Those bastard detectives practically told me I'd be awaiting lethal injection if I didn't confess. Can you imagine being accused of a crime you had nothing to do with?"

"Yes."

"Oh, I'm so sure. And I can't imagine how they found out about Bob Greenland making a pass at Talley. Or me talking about messing him up if he made a second pass at her. Did you really need to bring our family into that tragedy?"

I shrugged. "Part of my job," I said, choosing not to say I was sorry. I watched his hands carefully to see whether he was going to act on his anger. "It's not always pretty."

"I'm just glad it's over," he said, looking around and seeming to calm down before adding, "and I'll be glad when we don't see you around these parts."

I knew I'd be equally glad to not be coming back here again as well. But I simply shrugged again and said nothing. There was no point in engaging him further and exacerbating things. He had, after all, served in the Air Force.

The bleachers were now starting to get crowded, so finding seats far away from me was not an option. The Kingstons looked around, but finally decided to stay where they were, a row in front of me. With Noah Greenland back in uniform, the stands were now packed. Noah appeared apprehensive during warm-ups, the confident swagger he normally showed on the field was not in evidence. He was tentative in his throws. The team itself looked a bit lethargic. And as St. John Hershey roared onto the field, yelling and bouncing up and down, the St. Dismas Warriors looked, in comparison, very timid.

But then, as they say, things change. St. Dismas had the ball first and Noah lined up in the shotgun formation. On the first snap, he took the ball, got good protection, waited a couple of beats, and then fired a laser strike that Austin Bainbridge grabbed without breaking stride. The defender finally caught up with Austin and dragged him down on the 3 yard line. On the next play, Noah took one step back when he got the ball from center and lofted a pass deep in the corner of the end zone. Austin cut to the corner and, with arms outstretched, gathered it in. The cornerback was right there with him, but it was a perfect throw, the ball placed in the exact spot where only Austin could catch it, where no one else would be within reach. And it reminded me of an observation that one of the greatest quarterbacks in the history of the game had once said.

Many years ago, Johnny Unitas was leading his Colts team downfield for the winning score in an overtime NFL championship with the New York Giants. It was a match that some would call the greatest game ever played. The score was tied and the Colts had the ball inside the 10 yard line. All they needed to do was run the ball a few times and kick a winning field goal. But instead, Unitas threw what might have been considered a very risky sideline pass. Except that it was perfectly thrown, put right into the receiver's hands, and he went out of bounds on the 2 yard line. The Colts scored on the next play and Unitas was asked if he thought that sideline pass was dangerous, given that it might have been intercepted and could have changed the outcome of the game. He gave a response that was demonstrative of a supremely confident leader. Unitas said it was only dangerous if you didn't know what the hell you were doing. And as I watched Noah Greenland on this play, one thing was crystal clear. Noah knew exactly what he was doing. And it was equally clear that his confidence was beginning to return.

St. Dismas got the ball back a few minutes later, and they proceeded to do something which no one on the field expected. Noah took the snap and immediately threw the ball over to Austin, who had stepped back enough to ensure the pass was technically a backward lateral. Not expecting this, and not knowing quite what else to do, the defense reacted by racing toward him. Nearly everyone on the St. John Hershey team surged forward to tackle Austin. Except Austin, of course, had no intention of running with the ball. He drifted back a few more steps and then heaved the ball to the other side of the field. And running uncovered, with no one within 20 yards of him, was Noah Greenland; the lanky body wearing number 4 was sprinting downfield all by himself. This play was called a double pass, which was two legal passes since one of them went backward. In football terms, because Austin had caught a backward lateral it meant he could still throw a perfectly legal forward pass. Noah had become an eligible receiver, a reality the opposition either didn't grasp, or just responded to very slowly.

As Noah looked back to gauge the flight of the ball, he found it, reached up, and plucked it out of the air easily. Slowing down, he literally danced into the end zone for another touchdown, with no defenders anywhere near him. Noah raised his arms, and both the crowd and his teammates roared jubilantly. His teammates were so excited that the entire 50-man roster left the sideline and flooded the end zone to join him. They mobbed Noah, causing the refs to immediately throw yellow flags all over the field. The St. John Hershey team stared in disbelief.

This wasn't something that typically happened in the first quarter, or even at the end of a typical game. But this was not a typical game. This marked the return of a deeply troubled, heartbroken kid, someone who had been smacked hard by some of the worst things life could dole out. It was an ugly storm that Noah had had to weather, and I knew from personal experience it would be a long slog for him to get back to dry ground. But it looked like he might be starting the process, and football might be his lifeboat, and perhaps even his ark. And as he ran back to the sidelines, his teammates patting and hugging him along the way, Noah pulled his gold helmet off. For a moment, brief and fleeting but noticeable nevertheless, I thought I saw Noah Greenland smile.

*

St. Dismas won the game handily, 49-10, and it wasn't as close as the score indicated. The double pass was a backbreaker, and you could literally see the air go out of the St. John Hershey team. I stayed around for a while after the game ended, congratulating some of the players and finally getting a chance to speak with Curly Underwood. I gave him a high-five rather than risk damaging any tendons with a handshake. He seemed, if not happy to see me, at least bemused.

"Burnside. You part of our fan base now?" he smiled.

"I suppose I am. Congratulations. On both the win and getting yourself a nice gig. Head football coach at a prominent prep school. Right place at the right time?"

"Something like that," he smiled as a parent came by, stopping only to pat the coach on the shoulder. "It's an interim position, but these things have a way of becoming permanent."

"So no more Duke Savich."

"Nope," Underwood said. "It was his idea to recruit Noah, but Duke was the one who capitulated when Bob demanded money. Someone had to take responsibility, and Duke was the one who gave the thumbs up here. High school is a different world now."

"Apparently. I coached college for three years. There were always rumors that certain schools paid the players or their families. But it rarely gets divulged, and it's rarer still to have checks drawn."

"Savich was sloppy," he said. "If he were smart he would have just delivered a few suitcases full of cash. No footprints."

"That your plan?" I asked.

Underwood shook his head. "Those days are over. We're running a clean program now. Have to. Public scrutiny will demand it."

"Not to mention the fact that players like Noah Greenland come along about every 40 years."

"Maybe so."

"What's Savich going to do now?" I asked.

Curly Underwood smiled, held his palms up in a who-cares signal, and then tried to duck as a group of players doused him with what was left of a bucket of light green Gatorade. He laughed, told them they would be doing extra laps on Monday, and waved goodbye to me as he trotted off to the locker room, drops of green fluid falling off of him as he went. I took one last look around the St. Dismas field, headed to my Pathfinder and drove home in the darkness.

The next day was Saturday, and I normally didn't go into the office on a weekend. But Gail and Marcus were off to a Mommy and Me class, and Chewy was still snoring away at 8:30 a.m. And when I checked my voice mail, I heard a message that got my attention immediately. The caller didn't leave a name, and their voice was only vaguely recognizable. They said they needed my help, and they had nowhere else to turn. They asked if I would be in the office Saturday morning, but did not leave a phone number for me to get back to them. Intriguing did not describe this so much as insanely compelling.

The morning was sunny, but there were a few puffy clouds gathering overhead. I arrived at my office at 9:00 am, a *grande* cup of Starbucks Pike Place Blend in hand. The caffeine jolt was nice. I sat in my office, sipping coffee, my mind wandering back to the pain that kids like Noah Greenland and Dash Farsakian were going through. This was a part of me I could not control, the part that sympathizes with kids who had not received a fair deal in life. I never knew my father; he died in a car accident before I was born. Whatever pain I had from that loss lay deep inside of me, and it didn't surface much, only when I came upon someone whose pain might surpass mine. When I was a kid, the only time it bothered me was when I saw a friend spending time with his father. I tried not to dwell on it, but that hole in my heart was always there.

Having put in thirteen years with the LAPD, I saw so many examples of what not to do as a parent. I don't know if that was good training for fatherhood, but it at least showed me some potholes to avoid. Parenting involved sacrifice, but if you loved your child, there really wasn't much to give up. I didn't have a roadmap; I simply tried to be a good dad to Marcus. Or as good a dad as I knew how to be.

These thoughts came full circle when I heard a soft knock on my office door. I told them to come in and the knob turned and the door opened slowly. The person who entered had the same sad eyes I had seen so many times before in my career. A person in desperate need of help. They didn't need to verbalize it, the look of pain and fear and panic and despair were so clearly evident. But this was a little different from all the others. The pain they brought with them, would include my own.

She sat down quietly. Her long blonde hair hung down, slightly unkempt, unwashed for a few days, but still had that golden glow. She had been crying recently, the tip of her nose was red, and her mouth was twisted in a crooked way. Her eyes were watery, but they were still big and blue.

It had been almost ten years since I had seen her. She no longer exuded the innocence of a teenage waif. She was still attractive, but her beauty had hardened over the years. Her appearance still cried out that she was someone in need of protection. I steeled myself. I did not want to fall for this again. The last time had cost me, hugely, unfairly, and had changed my life in an unalterable way. I didn't want my life to change any more. But I did need to get closure on this particular chapter of it. Maybe Judy Atkin did as well.

"Let me start," she said with a slight sniffle, "by saying, I'm really, really, really sorry for what happened."

"Me, too."

"I heard you got kicked off the LAPD."

"Yes," I said. "A long time ago."

"I made a big mistake," she said, looking down at the floor.

"Yes."

She hesitated. "But I need your help. I've got a big problem. I don't know where else to turn."

I looked at Judy Atkin for a long moment and began to seriously consider that bad things actually did come in threes. I swiveled in my chair and looked out the window. The sky was still blue, and the sun was still shining. But the large clouds off on the horizon were growing bigger.

The End

## About The Author

David Chill was born and raised in New York City and educated in the public schools. After receiving his undergraduate degree from SUNY-Oswego, he moved to Los Angeles where he earned a Masters degree from the University of Southern California. David Chill is the author of seven mystery novels: *Post Pattern, Fade Route, Bubble Screen, Safety Valve, Corner Blitz, Nickel Package, Double Pass* and *Tampa Two,* all featuring Burnside, a private investigator and former LAPD officer and college football star. He is also the author of *Curse Of The Afflicted*, a political suspense novel which chronicles the journey of a political pollster diagnosed with cancer.

*Post Pattern* was a finalist in the St. Martin's Press contest for New Private Eye Mystery Writers. The Burnside series has received much critical acclaim, and all of his novels have spent time on the Amazon.com best seller lists. David Chill currently lives in Los Angeles with his wife and son. If you would like to contact David Chill directly, please email him at the following: davidchill3214@gmail.com

www.ingramcontent.com/pod-product-compliance
Lightning Source LLC
Chambersburg PA
CBHW020608260626
47157CB00003B/917